"We Could Meet In The Boardroom And Have Access To The Conference Table."

A burst of heat shot through Zach at the thought of what he would like to do with Erin on top of that table. That bothered him. He suspected Erin was the kind of woman who could make him reveal his darkest secrets.

"What time?"

"Six."

"Good. I'll bring dinner. What do you like?"

"Spicy," she said.

If she only knew what she was doing to him, she'd probably prefer to walk back. But maybe not. Maybe she did inject passion into everything she attempted. Something told him he just might have to find out.

Dear Reader,

Welcome to Silhouette Desire, the ultimate treat for Valentine's Day—we promise you will find six passionate, powerful and provocative romances every month! And here's what you can indulge yourself with this February....

The fabulous Peggy Moreland brings you February's MAN OF THE MONTH, *The Way to a Rancher's Heart*. You'll be enticed by this gruff widowed rancher who must let down his guard for the sake of a younger woman.

The exciting Desire miniseries TEXAS CATTLEMAN'S CLUB: LONE STAR JEWELS continues with *World's Most Eligible Texan* by Sara Orwig. A world-weary diplomat finds love—and fatherhood—after making a Plain Jane schoolteacher pregnant with his child.

Kathryn Jensen's *The American Earl* is an office romance featuring the son of a British earl who falls for his American employee. In *Overnight Cinderella* by Katherine Garbera, an ugly-duckling heroine transforms herself into a swan to win the love of an alpha male. Kate Little tells the story of a wealthy bachelor captivated by the woman he was trying to protect his younger brother from in *The Millionaire Takes a Bride*. And Kristi Gold offers *His Sheltering Arms*, in which a macho ex-cop finds love with the woman he protects.

Make this Valentine's Day extra-special by spoiling yourself with all six of these alluring Desire titles!

Enjoy!

Joan Marlow Golan

Joan Marlow Golan
Senior Editor, Silhouette Desire

Please address questions and book requests to:
Silhouette Reader Service
U.S.: 3010 Walden Ave., P.O. Box 1325, Buffalo, NY 14269
Canadian: P.O. Box 609, Fort Erie, Ont. L2A 5X3

His Sheltering Arms
KRISTI GOLD

Silhouette Desire

Published by Silhouette Books

America's Publisher of Contemporary Romance

SILHOUETTE BOOKS

ISBN 0-373-76350-6

HIS SHELTERING ARMS

Books by Kristi Gold

Silhouette Desire

Cowboy for Keeps #1308
Doctor for Keeps #1320
His Sheltering Arms #1350

KRISTI GOLD

began her romance-writing career at the tender age of twelve, when she and her sister spun romantic yarns involving a childhood friend and a popular talk-show host. Since that time, she's given up celebrity heroes for her favorite types of men—doctors and cowboys—as her husband is both. An avid sports fan, she attends football and baseball games in her spare time. She resides on a small ranch in central Texas with her three children and retired neurosurgeon husband, along with various livestock ranging from Texas longhorn cattle to spoiled yet talented equines. At one time she competed in regional and national Appaloosa horse shows as a non-pro, but she gave up riding for writing and turned the "reins" over to her youngest daughter. She attributes much of her success to her sister, Kim, who encouraged her in her writing, even during the tough times. When she's not in her office writing her current book, she's dreaming about it. Readers may contact Kristi at P.O. Box 11292, Robinson, TX 76116.

To Leigh Riker—long before I called you my friend,
you were my inspiration. Now I am twice blessed.

To those who have left their abusive partners
to find a better life,
I honor your courage and dedicate this book to you.
And to the women who have lost their battle
in the domestic violence war, may we never forget you.

Special acknowledgment goes to
Sharon Benner and Family Violence Prevention Fund
for their invaluable insight and information.

One

He wore his all-American good looks like a merit badge, but the devil in his dark eyes told Erin Brailey this man was no Boy Scout.

Zach Miller strode through Erin's office door with an athletic grace that immediately captured her imagination. Although some might deem his appearance inappropriate for a business meeting, she appreciated his chambray shirt and jeans. The clothes fit as if tailor-made to showcase his attributes.

But no matter how perfect his layered black hair, how breathtaking his six-foot-plus frame, she refused to allow his presence to distract her. This was business. Maybe the most important business of her life.

She stepped to the side of her desk and offered him her hand and a smile. "Mr. Miller, I'm Erin Brailey, executive director of Rainbow Center. Thanks for coming in."

"I'm glad to meet you, Ms. Brailey." His strong, callused hand gripped hers, complementing the rough timbre of his voice.

After he released her hand, Erin reclaimed her desk chair and motioned for him to take the seat across from her. Once he settled in, she flipped open a folder and scanned the information inside. "I guess you know we've accepted your bid."

"Not until now."

When she looked up, he was watching her, his bent elbow resting on the chair arm, finger and thumb forming an L-shaped support for his head from temple to jaw. His casual posture didn't detract from his air of control.

Erin consulted the material again to avoid his steady scrutiny. She brushed her hair from her face and caught a whiff of his heady cologne lingering on her fingertips. "Since the center decided not to go public with sealed bids, I assumed we'd have to pay more for security." After closing the file, she folded her hands in front of her and met his gaze.

He leaned forward, his espresso eyes boring into her. "If you're worried about getting your money's worth, I guarantee you'll be completely satisfied."

Although his expression didn't change, Erin's composure slipped a notch. If any other contractor had told her the same thing, she wouldn't have given the words a second thought. But coming from this great-smelling man with the whisky voice and sinful eyes, she felt like the target of a drive-by, indecent proposal. One she might be tempted to accept.

Shaking the ridiculous thoughts from her brain, Erin loosened her joined hands from their death grip and fought the urge to turn the thermostat down to sixty. The center couldn't afford the extra electricity. Neither could she.

"I'm not worried about the quality of your work," she

said. "You come highly recommended by Gil Parks, and I trust his judgment. I'm simply trying to understand your motivation for accepting a job that might show little profit for your company."

Zach sat back and scrubbed at his jaw with one hand. "Are you expecting an 'I'm serving my community' speech?"

Erin tamped down the surge of anger. Long ago she had come to realize that not everyone was committed to the shelter and the issues it represented. "I'm expecting an honest answer."

His lazy gaze took in the surroundings, the olive-green curtains, the marred oak desktop, the yellowed walls. He finally brought his eyes back to her. "I did my homework, Ms. Brailey. I know there's a need for this new shelter. You can't be too careful about the causes you support financially."

She supposed she should be flattered he'd chosen to bestow his selective altruism on Rainbow Center, but her cautious nature jumped into autopilot. "Phase II has been chosen to assist some of the larger municipalities because of its rural location. It will provide a totally secure environment dependent on private protection. We will require the utmost discretion since it's designed to provide refuge for women whose batterers are high-profile or work within service occupations in the surrounding communities."

"You mean cops."

"Yes, law enforcement does fall under that umbrella along with paramedics, firemen and anyone else who would know the whereabouts of the existing shelters in their area. The house isn't registered under the center's name. Neither are the utilities. So for all intents and purposes, it will appear to be an isolated farmhouse sitting in

the middle of seventy-five acres. But we'll still require
private security since nothing is 100 percent foolproof.''

"That makes sense.''

Something about Zach Miller's frown bothered Erin.
"So, have you always worked in security?''

He shifted in the chair and rubbed one large hand down
his jeans-clad thigh. "No. I used to be a cop.''

Warning bells rang out in Erin's brain. As the center's
staff accountant, Gil Parks was usually meticulous. Not
this time. *Before* Gil invited Zach Miller's bid and convinced the board of directors to accept it, he should have
brought this significant detail to Erin's attention immediately despite the fact Zach was a long-time acquaintance
and trusted friend of Gil's. She was governed by the
board—respected community leaders—and she'd worked
hard to build their trust. She wouldn't allow an error in
judgment to destroy their faith in her and compromise the
project. She had to know more about Zach Miller.

"How long were you in law enforcement?'' she asked,
trying to keep the concern from her voice.

"Twelve years total. Seven with Dallas PD, five right
here in Langdon. I've been in the security business for
three.''

"Why did you leave the department?''

"Burnout.'' Some unnamed emotion flared in his dark
eyes, but it disappeared as quickly as it came.

Erin made a mental note to ask Gil for more details
about Zach Miller's departure from the force. "Do you
still have contact with your former colleagues?''

"A few.''

Feeling a headache coming on, Erin pinched the bridge
of her nose. "I hope this isn't going to be a problem.''

"What do you mean?''

She squared her shoulders and looked at him straight

on. "I know it's rare, especially in a community the size of Langdon, but should the situation arise, are you going to be able to provide protection for beaten wives and girl-friends of law enforcement colleagues, then keep it a secret?"

He leaned forward, his dark eyes boring into her. "Are you asking can you trust me?"

"Yes. That's exactly what I'm asking."

He remained the portrait of restraint, but Erin noted a flash of anger pass over his face. "Ms. Brailey, I have no problem protecting any woman from a man who thinks using her as a punching bag is his God-given right. Cop or no cop. And I've kept my share of secrets over the years."

She imagined he had. And probably still did.

He folded his arms across his broad chest and resumed a relaxed position. "You can trust me. So can your residents."

He hadn't raised his voice, but the conviction in his tone spoke volumes. And if her instincts were correct, Erin suspected he was much more than just a burned-out cop. She also wondered if he had more commitment to this project than he cared to admit. Only time would tell.

"I have to make sure we're clear on this issue," she said. "This is a pilot program. I have one more month to get it going. Our funding hinges on its success. If I can't make it work, then it's over before it gets a running start." She drew in a breath. "This shelter is very important to many people."

"And important to you?"

Her pride had given her away. "Yes. Me, too."

His grin came out of hiding. "Nothing wrong with that."

Erin smiled back and added perfect teeth to her covert

list of his assets, then scolded herself for doing just that. Yet she couldn't help but notice the sprinkling of crisp black hair peeking out from the opening in his shirt. She'd bet her meager salary he had a chest that wouldn't quit.

Zach Miller appeared to be a tough-around-the-edges man. A man her father would never approve of. Which made him all the more appealing to Erin. Unfortunately, he would have to remain off-limits. She didn't have time for men. Or maybe she just didn't have the fortitude to explore the possibilities, considering past experience. Although at the moment the thought was tempting.

"Ms. Brailey?"

Her face flamed when she realized he'd been speaking. "I'm sorry. Just daydreaming."

"Must've been one heck of a daydream." His grin deepened, revealing a single dimple at the left corner of his mouth. A nice spot to kiss, Erin decided.

Bolting from her chair, Erin sent the papers on her desk into a frenzied dance. "That about does it. I guess we're settled and ready for you to get started."

His smile faded, but it didn't detract from his brooding good looks. "Aren't you coming with me?"

Her pulse did the cha-cha. "Where?"

"The new shelter. I worked the bid from a blueprint, so I haven't actually seen it yet. If you have the time, I can show you some of what I have in mind."

Thank heavens he didn't know what she'd had in mind a minute ago. "You mean now?"

"Now is good for me."

If she thought he wouldn't notice, Erin would kick herself in the backside with her black pumps for sounding so unnerved. "Sure. There's nothing here that can't wait."

Erin slipped her blazer on and grabbed her purse. Zach followed her to the reception desk where she addressed the college student filling in for the summer. "Cathy, Mr. Miller and I are going to visit the new shelter." She consulted her watch while the receptionist stared at Zach. "I may not be back, so forward all important calls to my home or page me."

"Yes, ma'am," Cathy said as she brought her gaze briefly to Erin, then back to Zach.

Erin headed toward the exit wondering if Cathy had heard a word she'd said. Obviously, the man had the same effect on women eighteen to sixty and all points in between.

Luckily, Erin had grown immune to men too handsome for their own good. At least she thought she had. Until today.

Silence hung over the cab of the truck like the dust rising off the dash as Zach skirted one rural pothole after another. He hadn't quite gotten over the impact of meeting Erin Brailey, five feet eight inches of pure fantasy—blond hair, blue eyes, with a body that could stop a high-stakes game of poker. Right now she afforded him a good view of her thighs where her tight black skirt had ridden up. He reminded himself to focus on the road and keep his libido in check.

In his peripheral vision, Zach saw Erin shimmy out of her jacket. He also noticed the way the white satin blouse clung to her round breasts. He tightened his grip on the steering wheel.

"Are you hot?" he asked with a cursory glance in her direction. He certainly was.

"It's a little warm," she answered. "Looks like it's going to be a blistering Texas summer if May's any indication."

Small talk. He could handle that. "I'll turn up the air."

When he set the control all the way to high, a burst of cold air blew into his face, but it didn't do much for the heat her presence had generated in his uncooperative body.

"How much farther?" he asked.

"Turn right in two miles, then it's another eight."

He started to ask how they chose the site, but his words died when he glimpsed her breasts again. Now she was cold. He silently cursed the fact the shelter was still ten minutes away.

Clearing the uncomfortable hitch in his throat, he asked, "How long have you been working for Rainbow Center?"

When she crossed her arms over her chest, Zach was both disappointed and relieved. "I've been with the center since I started college," she said. "I worked my way up to director while I completed my graduate studies."

"In counseling?"

"I have an MBA. I have a pretty good head for business."

She had a pretty good body to go right with it.

Damn! He needed to get a grip. This was business; she represented a client. Try telling that to his testosterone.

He shifted in the seat. "Public service is a bitch, though. Lousy pay, long hours. With your credentials, have you thought about finding a more lucrative job?"

When she didn't immediately answer, he glanced her way again. The look she gave him could melt the tires out from under his truck. "Something wrong?" he asked.

"If you mean that my job is a waste of my talents, I assure you that what I do matters. If you'd ever looked into the eyes of the child of a batterer, then you'd know what I mean."

"Believe me, Ms. Brailey, I have." He'd been that child.

She shot him a remorseful look, then shook her head.

"I'm sorry. I'm sure you have. I'm just a little testy when it comes to defending my reasons for staying with the shelter."

"I was just speaking from personal experience." But he wasn't so jaded that he didn't know exactly where she was coming from. Dealing with kids who were victims of adult brutality had never been easy. In fact, it had torn at his heart and had nearly destroyed his faith in humanity. People like Erin Brailey were few and far between. She reminded him that good did exist in this screwed-up world. And he admired her for her commitment, her passion for the cause. If only he could feel that way again—the way he'd felt before it had all come apart.

Zach didn't know what to say or if he should just keep his mouth shut. He couldn't help but wonder if Erin Brailey's passion carried over into her personal life. Was she as all-fired enthusiastic about other things?

He might as well get "other things" out of his head if he wanted to remain objective. No problem. Control was one of his stronger suits. Under normal circumstances.

A few minutes later the truck crunched up the gravel drive leading to the shelter. The gate hung askew, the paint on the white frame house was blistering and peeling. Someone had finished painting the front facade but not all the way up to the second floor. From the looks of things, another month might not be enough time to get the place in shape.

Zach barely put the truck into park before Erin opened the door and slid out. As he watched her walk toward the entrance, he realized she looked as good in back as she did in front. He got out of the truck muttering a litany of curses and cautions.

Zach entered the shelter but didn't immediately see Erin. His booted heels echoed in the hall as he walked the well-worn hardwood floor. At the end of the foyer he found Erin at the bottom of the stairs surveying a freshly painted wall.

"This is looking much better." She faced him with a polite smile. "The bottom floor consists of mainly the manager's quarters, a kitchen, a living room and a small den. All the bedrooms are upstairs. Where do you want to start?"

He surveyed the surroundings, noting some places that looked vulnerable to a security breach. "Down here's fine."

"Okay." She glanced up the stairs, then turned back to him. "You can start here, and I'll be with you in a minute. If you don't mind, I want to check on the second-floor children's room and make sure it's been done right."

The sudden softening of her features took Zach by surprise, and then he recalled her earlier comment about the kids. "The children's room, huh?"

Her smile was almost self-conscious, as if she'd been caught in some illicit act. "Don't look so shocked, Mr. Miller. I admit I like kids. I work with them at the shelter with a self-esteem program. It's important to break the cycle before they reach adulthood."

"I understand." More than she would ever know. Zach made a sweeping gesture toward the stairs. "By all means check it out. You can join me down here when you're done."

"Thanks. I'll be back in a while."

After Erin departed up the stairs, Zach got busy surveying the rooms, checking the windows, making notes about his concerns. He listed all points of vulnerability and completed the initial evaluation and still he had yet to see Erin again. Although he would need to return at least one more time before getting started on the wiring, in case he missed something, he was pretty much finished evaluating the first floor. Might as well go find Ms. Brailey.

He headed toward the staircase, shaking his head. Erin Brailey liked kids. He wouldn't have guessed that about her, but then his instincts about women weren't always correct. Those who appeared the toughest on the surface often hid their vulnerabilities from the world. He'd learned that the hard way. But Erin Brailey wasn't a victim.

Zach gripped the rickety banister and took the stairs two at a time. When he reached the top landing, the acrid smell of fresh paint assaulted his nostrils and burned his eyes. He moved down the hall, glancing into each room, one newly renovated, the other waiting its turn. He paused to consider what a place like this would have meant to his mother. Maybe things would have been different if she'd had the resources to change her life for the better. Maybe he would have been different. But that was the past, something Zach couldn't alter.

Continuing on, Zach found Erin in the third room beyond the staircase, a small bedroom decorated in a pastel blue with yellow rabbits bordering the wall where it met the ceiling. Normally he wouldn't notice what the room looked like, but Erin Brailey's fitted skirt contrasted with the walls like black leather against a backdrop of sky. She was standing on the top rung of a ladder in her stocking feet, reaching up where a piece of the bunny border had obviously come undone.

He could very well come undone if she didn't get down off the blasted ladder. He had the strongest urge to go to her, run his hands up the sides of her sculpted thighs…

Hold it right there, Miller. He streaked a hand over his eyes as if that could erase the image. Man, oh, man, he was in trouble. He should get out of here, go to his favorite bar and find himself a woman. Easier said than done. Erin

Brailey, with the soft spot for kids and no-holds-barred confidence, held more appeal than any woman he could think of, past or present.

"Need some help?" he asked.

She regarded him over her shoulder. "No…I'm just about done." She smoothed the border with one long tapered hand, then slapped it for good measure. "There. Good as new."

She backed down the rungs and once she reached the bottom, turned to face him. Using the ladder for balance, she slipped her heels back on and asked, "Did you get a good look?"

Hell, had he been that obvious? "At what?"

"Downstairs. Did you see what you wanted to?"

At the moment he'd seen much more than he'd wanted to. Correction. Needed to. "Yeah. So if you're through hanging paper, you could show me around up here."

She brushed a few golden strands of hair away from her face with one hand. "I'm through for now."

"Is paper hanging in your job description, too?"

"Not exactly, but we're lacking in volunteers. Considering the nature of this project, the fewer people who know the location, the better."

"I'm pretty handy with a brush. Maybe I could help."

Erin took two steps forward and studied him with eyes as blue as the sky blue walls. "I'm sure you have better ways to spend your time than painting an old house."

"Actually, I don't. After business hours, at least."

She raised a thin brow. "Your wife wouldn't mind?"

"I don't have a wife." Since she had broached the subject, he might as well ask. "How about you? Husband?"

She twisted the ring on her right hand. "Heavens, no."

"Sorry subject?"

She brushed past him and stopped at the door. "You

know how it is, Mr. Miller. Priorities don't always include the husband, two-point-five kids and a golden retriever.''

He moved to stand opposite her and braced a hip against the door frame. ''Yeah, I know what you mean. But surely you don't spend all your time at work.''

''Lately, yes. I haven't found anything that captures my passion like my work.''

''Or anyone?''

''No. Definitely not,'' she said adamantly.

Zach clenched the back of his neck with one hand and studied the semiwhite drop cloth under his feet. ''That's a shame, Ms. Brailey. A real shame.''

''Don't feel sorry for me, Mr. Miller. I manage.''

Pity didn't enter into it. She wasn't the kind of woman a man felt sorry for. He met her gaze. Big mistake. ''It's Zach, and since neither of us seems to be occupied, do you want to grab a bite to eat? I could go over a few of my concerns.''

She sighed. ''That sounds very tempting, but I'm afraid I have dinner plans. He's probably already at the restaurant.''

A strong sense of disappointment assaulted Zach, not that he was one to give up that easily. He leaned forward and lowered his voice. ''Someone special?''

''Actually, I'm having dinner with my father.''

He straightened on that one. ''You and your dad are close?''

In the time it took to blink, her expression went cold. ''It's an obligatory weekly dinner. That's all.''

Zach wondered about the sudden change in her demeanor but thought it wise not to pursue the topic. He understood all too well the complicated dynamics between parent and child. He'd hated his father and still did, even though the man was dead.

"My father doesn't like to be kept waiting," she added. "So let's go down the hall, Mr.—" Her mouth worked into a smile "—Zach."

She could make St. Peter sin with that smile. Which, as a practiced sinner, made Zach a goner. "At least we have the name thing straight. And let's make another deal. We say what's on our minds, no apologies. I think that works best with business arrangements." He held out his hand. "Is it a deal?"

After a moment's hesitation, she grasped his hand. "Deal."

He didn't immediately release her hand. Instead, he rubbed his thumb over her knuckles and met her eyes, surprise in their blue depths. Awareness sparked between them, keen as a razor's edge.

Checking back into reality, he dropped her hand. "Better wear gloves when you paint so you don't ruin your hands."

She studied her hands as if she didn't believe him. "Thanks for the advice, but I'm not that fragile."

No, she probably wasn't, but he'd give up a week's salary to find out. He might even throw in his season hockey tickets.

Zach pushed off the door thinking he'd best escape before he did something stupid. "Well, Ms. Brailey—"

"It's Erin. Turnabout's fair play."

He grinned. "Okay, Erin, we should look around so you're not late for your dinner date."

"You're right. Can't keep Daddy waiting." Her tone was laced with sarcasm.

They walked the hall, and before they reached the next room, Erin turned back to him. "Since this tour is going to have to be quick, why don't you come by my office tomorrow? You can bring the blueprint and show me your ideas."

Zach slipped his hands into his pockets, all too eager to accept. "Morning okay?"

"I'm afraid it will have to be later. I visit the other shelter in the mornings, and I have a board meeting at four-thirty. You could meet me after that in the boardroom. That way we'll have access to the conference table."

A burst of heat shot through him at the thought of what he would like to do with her on top of that table. The image came to him sharp and clear and totally unexpected. What was it about her that had his fantasies running away with his common sense? It was physical, yes, but there was more. That bothered him. He could control animal lust, but he didn't like to deal with human need. He suspected Erin was the kind of woman who could make him reveal his darkest secrets, if he wasn't careful. He couldn't afford to open old wounds. "What time?"

She started back down the hall. "Six."

Zach lagged behind so he could enjoy the view. "Good. I'll bring dinner. Chinese okay with you?"

"Great."

"What do you like?"

"Spicy," she said without turning around, but he detected a smile in her voice.

If she only knew what she was doing to him, she'd probably prefer to walk back. But maybe not. Maybe she did inject passion into everything she attempted. Something told him he just might have to find out.

Two

"**F**ifty thousand dollars, Erin? Fifty thousand is a great deal of money."

Erin sipped her wine and regarded her father over the bistro's elegant gold filigree candleholder situated perfectly on the round table for two. Although Robert Brailey's face was etched with fine lines, his neatly coifed hair now completely silver, he was still a handsome man. Even at sixty he looked much younger and every bit the prosperous politician. He'd retired two years before from his lengthy term in the state senate to reclaim his standing as a renowned corporate attorney. But the politico persona was as deeply ingrained as his love for the law, fine wine and classic cars. He wore the image well.

Erin grabbed the bottle of port and filled her glass, ignoring his disapproving stare. "I know it's a lot of money, but I need matching funds for this project. You have access to private donors." She tried to tamp down her desperation. "Because of the discretion involved, I can't go out into the community and solicit donations. You know people who can help."

He shoved his napkin aside. "You're wasting your talents staying in social service."

The muscles in Erin's shoulders ached from tension. Conversations with her father always came back to his disapproval of a job that he had deemed dead-end since the day she'd accepted the position. "You might as well face it. I'm not making a career change anytime soon."

"I'm well aware of that."

His glare caused her to sit back and knead her hands underneath the table like an errant child. But she refused to buckle. "If I can make this work, I'll achieve more satisfaction than any six-figure salary could provide."

"Satisfaction doesn't provide security."

"I have other rewards." For some reason Zach Miller came to mind. Obviously her hormones had run amok.

Her father cleared his throat, regaining her attention. "Until recently your greatest reward was your trust fund."

In that instant she wanted to hate him, but as always, she couldn't. Despite his attempts to run her life, he was still her father. She'd inherited her conviction from him, along with a good dose of stubbornness. At the moment, she needed his influence, and she would do anything, even grovel, to get it. For the shelter, she would swallow her pride.

Erin gently touched his hand. "Will you help me?"

He slid his hand from beneath hers and patted her arm. His well-rehearsed smile meant trouble. "I could investigate a few possibilities. On one condition."

She'd been mistaken to believe that his help would come without conditions. Her sigh rose over the background hum of dinnertime conversation. "What condition?"

He took a long drink of wine and dabbed at his mouth with a mauve linen napkin. "How long will it take you to get this new shelter up and running?"

"We want to open in a month."

"And how long to ensure its continuity?"

"If we can make a successful go of it for a year, that should convince the board it's a worthwhile project."

"I see." He raised a hand to wave at some patron Erin didn't recognize but continued to speak without missing a beat. "And if you don't succeed, what then?"

She didn't want to consider that possibility, although it was sheer stupidity not to. "We'll continue business as usual with the existing shelter. We'll just have to relocate our at-risk residents to other shelters and safe houses."

He sat in silence for a moment longer—she assumed to consider his choice of weapons. She braced for his best shot.

"I'll agree to help find your funding," he said, "if you agree to consider coming to work for me if you fail."

Gritting her teeth, she suppressed the urge to blurt out her refusal. She would be damned and desperate before she'd work for his firm under the guise of administrator, when in reality she'd be nothing more than a glorified hostess. Since her mother's death twelve years before, he'd told her often enough he needed her in that capacity. And since her breakup with Warren, the perfect son-in-law prospect, her father never failed to remind her—not always so subtly—how great a disappointment she had been. Nothing had changed. Except Erin.

Now, more than ever, she was determined to succeed and prove him wrong. "If I do agree, would you promise to use all your resources to find the funds?"

"Are you asking would I set you up to fail?"

"It is a concern, don't you think?"

He had never let Erin forget her former failures. Mistakes made by a rebellious sixteen-year-old girl who'd lost her mother. A teenager in desperate need of her father's attention. Erin had gotten his attention and earned his distrust.

Robert's face turned as stoic as the fake Roman bust in the corner. "I'll give you my word, if that's good enough."

For a moment she felt ashamed. But the moment was short-lived. She needed his help, whatever his terms. She had no choice but to trust him.

Erin gathered all her inner strength and said the words she never thought she would say. "I agree to your proposal."

Shock passed over his expression, but it didn't take long for him to remold his face into a picture-perfect model of dignity. "Then you'll come to work for me?"

"*If* the project doesn't succeed."

His shoulders relaxed and a victorious smile crept in. "What made you agree to my condition?"

Erin stood to make her escape. She wasn't going to waste her time explaining how much the center meant to her. Or exactly how far she'd go to ensure its success. "Well, Father, it's simple." She took her purse from the back of her chair and slipped the braided strap over her shoulder. Then she produced a determined look designed to complement her parting words.

"I'm not going to fail."

Erin left the boardroom the next afternoon in a state of euphoria. As the board members filtered out, she was met with congratulations and optimism. For the first time since she'd proposed the new shelter, she believed it was going to work.

After the last of the requisite goodbyes, she noticed a figure standing near the vacant reception desk. Cathy had gone home for the day, but the door hadn't been locked in order to allow the board members to exit. The stranger wore a plain dark suit and his sandy hair close cropped. The shiny plastic-covered Langdon PD credentials pinned to his lapel contrasted his dull-gray eyes. She had met several men from the local department, all very nice and accommodating, but she didn't recognize this man.

Erin approached the desk slowly, a sense of foreboding settling over her with each click-clack of her heels hitting the industrial-tiled floor. The shelter was situated a block away from the center. Normally, when there was trouble, she'd receive a call from the on-duty house manager. Maybe he wasn't here on official business, but the determined look on his ruddy face indicated this wasn't a social call.

Erin donned her professional smile. "May I help you?"

He was close to her height, but his deportment seemed almost predatory. "Are you Miss Brailey?"

"Yes, I'm *Ms*. Brailey."

"Detective Andrews, Langdon PD," he announced, without the offer of a handshake. "I need to speak to you immediately."

Erin glanced at the desk clock. Zach Miller was due anytime now, but the tone in the detective's voice told her that his business couldn't wait. Or at least he thought it couldn't. "I have an appointment, but I can give you a few minutes. Come on into my office."

She led the way and, once inside, positioned herself behind the desk. She gestured to the chair Zach had occupied the day before. "Have a seat."

"I'll stand."

Erin remained standing, as well, to maintain an equal advantage. "What can I do for you, Detective?"

His steely gaze darted around the room before finally coming to rest on Erin. "It's about this new shelter you're planning. The grapevine says it's a house for cops' wives."

Erin had suspected word would get out sooner or later. She'd hoped for later. "If that situation arises. Is there a problem?"

"The problem is some of us don't like it. Makes the department look bad, you know what I mean? Bad PR for police."

Erin gripped the back of her chair. "Actually, Detective, the proposed shelter is not targeted solely at the partners of those in law enforcement. There is a need for a safe house for women abused by anyone that would know the existing shelter's whereabouts, in Langdon and in the surrounding suburbs, including the larger cities. Our intent is not to belittle police departments. In fact, we rely heavily on their services at our existing shelter."

His laugh was abrupt, humorless. "No kidding. Our guys risk their necks getting involved in domestic fights. Can't even tell you how many times when I was still working the streets I had a jealous husband threaten me. We go in there and break up their lovers' quarrel only to have the woman bail him out the next day. People need to learn to settle their problems on their own. It's an ever-lovin' pain in the butt."

No matter how much time the center had devoted to education, a select few still didn't understand the dynamics of abuse. This man was a prime example.

Erin's patience left the building. "No kidding," she said, throwing his words back at him. "For the women it's a big pain in the butt. And sometimes, the arms, the nose and so forth.''

He balled his fists at his side, his round face flushing an unnatural shade of red. ''Why don't you leave well enough alone? You've got one place for them, why do you need another?''

She straightened up to her full height, refusing to be intimidated by a man with questionable motives, even if he did wear a badge. ''Because some men don't understand that it's against the law to hit their wives or girlfriends. Those wives and girlfriends need a place where no one can get to them.''

''Cops can go anywhere they want.''

''Not if they're stopped.''

He gave her a sickening once-over, then smirked. ''And who's going to stop them? You?''

Erin opened her mouth to respond but was stopped short by a deep, controlled voice. A voice full of hatred. A voice belonging to Zach Miller.

''I will.''

Tension as thick as a winter fog settled over the small office. Neither man moved, as if facing off for a duel.

Zach tightened his grasp on the rolled blueprint he clutched in one hand. ''What do you want, Andrews?''

The sour apple look on the detective's face repulsed Erin. ''This is business, Miller. And it's none of yours.''

Zach took another step forward. ''Yeah, well I don't intend to involve myself in your business. Unless I have to.''

''Good. At least you've learned your place.''

''But I doubt you have.''

Erin watched Zach's features harden as if the last vestiges of his control were slipping away. She couldn't let that happen, so she moved from behind the desk and said,

"Detective Andrews, Mr. Miller is my next appointment, so if you're through now—" she headed to the door and held it open "—I'll see you out."

"Don't bother," Andrews retorted. "I can find my way."

The detective strode past Zach with an acid glare. Erin closed the door behind him and leaned back against it.

Zach stood in the middle of the room with a choke hold on the blueprint as he stared at some focal point above her head.

Erin pushed off the door. "Old friend?"

He finally met her gaze, fury flashing in his dark eyes. "Old acquaintance. Not a friend."

Zach strolled around the room. Erin didn't speak, deciding to give him a moment to cool down.

He lifted a slat on the lone window's dusty miniblind and peered outside into the parking lot. "Why was he here?"

"He's curious about the new shelter."

Zach turned away from the window, his anger almost palpable. "How does he know about it?"

"Just because we keep the proposed site's whereabouts a secret doesn't mean we can keep its existence from the community. The surrounding police departments know about it. So does Langdon's police chief. We've always had a good rapport. I consider many of the men and women on the force good friends. In fact, almost all of them understand the need. Unfortunately, your *acquaintance* doesn't."

"That sure as hell isn't surprising."

Erin wanted to know why and exactly what Zach was hiding. What was his relationship with Andrews? More important, would it affect the new shelter? She walked to her desk and fumbled for a pencil and notebook. "What do you know about the detective?"

"Enough to know the bastard's trouble."

"I gather you two have a history."

Zach tapped the end of the desk with the blueprint. "Yeah, one I'm not willing to go into."

The intensity of his deep voice warned Erin not to press, even though she dearly wanted to. Eventually she would have to find an opportune time. But not now. Not while he was in such an agitated state. "Are you ready to get to work now?"

"Sure." He sent her a brief smile. "I left the food at the front desk. Where to?"

"The conference room."

Zach sat across from Erin at the mile-long table and stared at his food. Today Ron Andrews had ruined his appetite. Three years ago he'd ruined Zach's career. Every time he came in contact with Andrews, Zach was reminded of another ruthless man who also had been respected in his field. His own father.

As a successful physician, Vernon Miller should have been Zach's mentor. Instead he'd been his shame. Something Zach would have to live with for the rest of his life. Something that had colored his judgment during a time when he'd needed clear thinking the most. But he hadn't realized the error of his ways until it had been too late. Until he had failed another woman, just like he'd failed his mother.

"This is great."

Erin's comment drew Zach's attention back to her. He noticed she had no trouble eating. She wrapped her pretty mouth around an egg roll, waking another kind of hunger in his gut, bringing to mind all sorts of possibilities.

At least she served as a nice diversion from the earlier encounter. He wondered what she really thought about the confrontation, and then decided he didn't want to know. His past was his, and he didn't want to share it with anyone.

Zach pushed the recollections and food away, then stacked his hands behind his neck and leaned back in the chair. "Are you enjoying yourself?"

"Umm-hmm," she said around a bite of Szechwan chicken. "I didn't have time for lunch." She sipped from a foam cup of iced tea. "You didn't eat much."

"I'm not that hungry." At least not for food.

He expected her to make some comment about Andrews but instead she said, "I'm all done, so let's get to work."

A code of honor among police officers prevented him from revealing too much to her. To anyone. He appreciated the fact she didn't prod him for information. He appreciated a lot of things about Erin Brailey.

They cleared the red-and-white cartons away so Zach could roll the shelter's floor plan out onto the table. Erin anchored the blueprint at the corners with her beige briefcase, a spiral notebook and two stacks of Rainbow Center's trifold pamphlets.

Hands braced wide on the table, she leaned forward to study the plan. Zach stood behind her, the smell of her perfume drifting into his nostrils. The scent was pleasant, erotic. So was the dress she wore—sleeveless, high-necked, soft blue material that clung to every curve. A man-killing outfit. He should know. He was about to die right there on the spot.

After a good internal scolding, he leaned around her and pointed to the plan. "I'll set up two sensors here in the living room, wires on every window." He indicated the front door. "Key pad here. You can arm the system from this point, or in the back room where the resident manager stays.''

''What about outside?'' she asked.

''Motion lights.'' Despite his caution, he moved closer. Now almost flush against her back, his body paid the price. When he gestured at the plan again, their arms brushed, sending a rush of fire through him. If that's all it took, one simple touch, then he wondered if he'd survive kissing her. Why the hell he was considering that, he couldn't say. His thoughts had crossed into dangerous territory. Right now kissing her was foremost on his mind. Something to rid him of anger over the confrontation. Something to make him forget. But he needed to step back, proceed with caution.

''If there's a security breach and the guard needs backup, who will answer the call?'' she asked.

''I will.''

She straightened and looked over her shoulder, bringing their bodies into closer proximity and their faces only inches apart. She was so close. Too close for his comfort. He wasn't giving her much space. He didn't want to.

''What if you're busy?'' she asked, challenge in her tone.

Zach found it harder and harder to concentrate on business. Strong desire stirred down south, and he cautioned himself to maintain control. ''I carry a cell phone at all times. If I'm out of reach, one of my other men can handle it. But I don't plan on going anywhere anytime soon.''

The comment echoed in the room, suspending the moment. He inched back a step, giving his body some much-needed relief.

Erin turned her attention back to the plan. ''Upstairs?''

''The same. Sensors above and on the windows. And more motion-sensitive lights.''

"That's good. Night is a vulnerable time. But it's my favorite time."

He found himself moving closer again, her sultry voice drawing him like a magnet. "You're a night person, too?"

"If I could I'd stay up all night and sleep all day."

"So would I."

Electricity coursed through him and settled directly below his belt. He needed to get away from her soon, or he just might give in to some damned sinful ideas. But his feet seemed stapled to the floor, and he continued to lose himself in the sound of her sexy voice, at his body's expense.

"How do you spend your nighttime hours?" she asked, but still didn't turn around.

"TV, reading. Sometimes I pop open a beer and listen to my favorite jazz. And sometimes I cook." He'd never spoken so freely about his personal life with a woman. He'd learned not to reveal even that much of himself. But Erin Brailey was no ordinary woman.

Her laugh was full of surprise, not judgment. "You cook? That's great. I can't operate the microwave." She glanced back at him again. "Are you good?"

The way she said it made him wonder if the question had more to do with his performance in bed than his culinary talents. Probably just wishful thinking on his part. Either way, the answer was the same. "I'd like to think so."

She studied the plan again. "I'm sure you are."

Her whisper-soft words made him think of her in his arms, naked beneath him. "What do you do at night?" he asked.

"Nothing much. A cup of tea and a hot bath."

The image of Erin soaking in a tub did nothing to squelch his lust. "Alone?" *Careful, Miller.*

"I believe we've already established that."

"No one to scrub your back?"

"I have a brush. It does the trick."

The last thread of his control was badly frayed and ready to snap. Yet he didn't have the will to stop. "But it sure isn't as much fun as the real thing, is it?"

"That depends on what you mean by the 'real thing.'"

With every syllable she uttered, Zach's objectivity took another step toward the door, the excuse he needed to forget his responsibility. Forget why they were here and why he needed to steer clear. "Don't you get lonely, Erin?"

"Sometimes. A little." Only a partial truth, Erin acknowledged. She was more than a little lonely. She missed having someone to curl up with on the sofa, someone to have dinner with in front of the TV, the physical presence of a man. And, whether she cared to admit it or not, lovemaking.

But she didn't miss the emotional upheaval or the betrayal or the control. Still, she found herself wondering how far she was willing to go with a man like Zach Miller, a protector, something she didn't need. And a business associate to boot. But he made her feel alive. Feel things she had suppressed for months. Maybe she could indulge just a little, from a physical standpoint. As long as she guarded her heart.

Zach's warm breath trailed over her neck, and she shivered. "Are you cold?" he asked.

"Yes." *Liar.*

He stroked his palms down her bare arms, from shoulders to elbows, then back up again. She relaxed against him, relishing his gentle touch. The strength he radiated unearthed long-dormant carnal urges. "This is much better than a hot bath."

He brushed her hair aside and moved his lips to her ear. "Are you sure about this, Erin?"

"No. I'm only sure about one thing. I'm tired of talking."

"Then answer one more question. When was the last time you were kissed? I mean really kissed."

Her breath rode out on a sigh. "Too long."

"That's too bad."

He turned her around, and she met his midnight gaze, intense, hypnotic, seductive. As if in slow motion, he lowered his mouth to hers. She responded with a pent-up hunger that matched his urgency. She opened to him, accepted the play of his tongue as it entered her parted lips. The spicy taste of him staggered her senses, and a surge of heat charged through her, settling in places long neglected for lack of time or want.

Somewhere in the back of her mind she knew she should stop. Stop him. Stop herself. But she wanted this. More than she'd wanted anything in a long time. She would consider the consequences later. Right now she wanted to feel, not to think.

Disregarding the blueprint, Zach lifted Erin up and placed her on the edge of the table without leaving her eager mouth. He moved between her legs, parting them. She felt her skirt ride high up her thighs, way past the point of decency. Her mind reeled from the explosive chemistry that had destroyed her ability to reason, made her long for more. Here and now.

To her dismay Zach broke the kiss but kept his hands poised on her stocking-clad thighs and his dark gaze locked on her face. He inched his fingers under the hem, taking away her breath and her last bit of resolve.

"Tell me to stop, Erin."

The word formed in Erin's mind, then floated away like a delicate leaf caught in the wind.

Zach plied her neck with brushstroke kisses. "I want you, Erin. *Now.* So tell me to leave."

"No." She barely recognized her voice. She barely recognized herself.

With an animal groan Zach brought her hips forward to the edge of the table, and his mouth back to hers. Her awareness centered on his thumbs lightly stroking her thighs, his intoxicating kiss. The heavy pulse of desire washed her whole body in liquid heat, robbing her of all thoughts and protests.

Madness, she thought. Absolute madness that she would allow this to happen here, when anyone could walk in. But an uncontrollable need had brought them to this point. A place where only passion existed, away from past mistakes. For once Erin wanted to lose control.

Erin registered a sound filtering through the sensual haze. Then from somewhere far off came a rap at the door.

Three

"Erin, are you in there?"

Gil's familiar voice was ice water, dousing Zach's ardor. Running on instinct, Zach stepped back and helped Erin from the table. He pulled out a nearby chair and sat, needing to disguise the effect the spontaneous foreplay had on his body. He scooted the chair under the table and straightened the wrinkled blueprint as best he could, a reminder of his total loss of control. Erin Brailey was making him crazy.

In a flash Erin smoothed her dress and sent him a concerned look as she walked to the door. "Come in, Gil."

Gil Parks stepped inside the room wearing his standard blue suit and an accountant's expression. "I needed—" His glance went from Zach to Erin, then back to Zach. He pushed his wire-framed glasses up on the bridge of his nose. A knowing smile lifted his lips. "Miller, fancy meeting you here."

Zach sucked in a deep breath. "Gil, how's it going?"

"Fine. Don't get up."

Thank God for small favors. Zach couldn't stand if he wanted. Not without losing his dignity.

Zach shot a glance in Erin's direction. Her lips looked swollen and bruised from heated kisses. The red patch on her chin revealed the first signs of whisker burn. He had done that to her. That fact brought on another rush of excitement. Then came the guilt when he saw that the blush on her cheeks had faded, and she looked pale. His fault, too.

"Am I interrupting something?" Gil asked.

"Not really."

Erin's voice was amazingly calm, but Zach realized that only a fool wouldn't notice her appearance. Gil was no fool, but he was a good friend. Gil wouldn't say anything to embarrass either of them. Not in front of Erin, anyway.

"Ms. Brailey and I have been going over the security plans," Zach said, affecting nonchalance.

Gil stroked his bearded chin like a pet. "Ah. Did you get a lot accomplished?"

Erin brushed her hair away from her face with one hand. "Yes, but we're about ready to wrap it up. What did you need?"

"Actually, I have Zach's contract. Thought you might want to go over the financial aspects. Since he's here, I can review it with you both."

Erin grabbed for her briefcase. "You guys can work it out. I need to get home. Check my messages. Feed the cat."

Gil's smile was cynical. "You don't have a cat, Erin."

"That's right, I don't. But you never can tell when one might show up on your doorstep. I really need to go."

Zach stared at Erin. The little minx was bailing out on

him. "Yeah, you do that, Ms. Brailey. I'll talk to you tomorrow."

She strode toward the door. With a hand on the knob, she turned to face them both, but she looked at Zach. "Good night, Gil. And Mr. Miller, thanks for your time. See you around."

"Have a good night," Zach called as she headed out the door. "Enjoy your bath."

Erin sent him a don't-you-dare look as she closed the door.

Gil's chuckle echoed in the barren room. "Damn, Miller, you don't waste any time, do you?"

Zach decided playing dumb might be in his best interest. "There's not much time to get the security kinks worked out."

Gil leaned back against the table, arms crossed, legs stretched out in front of him. "Come off it. Erin's all business. Under normal circumstances she'd insist on going over the contract with a fine-tooth comb. Obviously she's all shook up. I have the distinct feeling that's your fault."

"She's in a hurry. Probably ready for bed."

"You both look ready for bed." Gil laughed again. "You and Erin Brailey. What a match. Sorry I didn't think of it."

"You been drinking, Gil?" Zach hated the fact he sounded so defensive. He'd always been good at hiding his emotions.

"Your secret's safe with me, Zach. But I tell you right now, you're playing with fire if you're playing with Erin."

He'd already been scorched. "How so?"

Gil pulled out another chair and tossed a folder onto the table. "She's a tough cookie. She comes from money. Big daddy used to be a state senator, and nothing's more important than his little girl. He probably eats her boyfriends for lunch.''

Zach streaked a hand over his face and cursed his stupidity. ''So Erin is the esteemed Robert Brailey's daughter. What else do you know about her? Personally, I mean.''

''She's driven, never been married. She did live with some guy for a while, an attorney in her father's firm. I'd say she's pretty much married to her work these days.''

That much Zach knew. ''Then she doesn't have a boyfriend.''

''No.'' Gil's lewd grin made another appearance. ''Are you intending to bid for that job, too?''

''No way.'' He didn't sound all that confident. ''I like her, but I don't do relationships.''

''No, my man, that you don't. I've known that since we were high school freshmen, and you were breaking all the girls' hearts on a regular basis. But in spite of her father, you couldn't do better than Erin. She's sexy as hell. Smart, too.''

''No kidding,'' Zach muttered. Yet tonight she hadn't been too smart. But then how would she know that staying away from him would be the best thing for both of them?

Gil's chuckle turned into a full-fledged laugh. ''Looks to me like she has you by the jewels, Miller.''

''Where's that damn contract?'' Zach asked, refusing to admit Gil Parks was right on the money. Erin had him all right, he just wasn't sure what she intended to do with him.

Erin had no idea what to do about him. She tossed and turned in bed, unable to clear her mind of Zach Miller.

Brushing her fingertips over her collarbone, she recalled the feel of his hands on her. His mouth on hers. Although the ceiling fan whirred above her and she wore nothing more than a frown, she might as well be decked out in a parka. She felt hot, restless, needy.

Rolling over, she buried her face in the satin-covered pillow. What had she been thinking to let things go so far? Better still, what did *he* think of her now?

She had never experienced such a total loss of restraint. She had never so much as held hands with anyone in a professional setting. Not even Warren. Not that Warren would have ever considered doing something so spontaneous. During their two years together, he had barely touched her in public. They had been professional people living professional lives. Somehow she had fallen in love with him, anyway, or at least she'd thought she had. He'd used that to his advantage, taking what she could give him—more accurately, what her father could give him—and then eventually left her behind when she couldn't live up to his ideal of the proper attorney's wife.

Zach seemed different. More down-to-earth. Strong and sensual. A man who knew how to kiss a woman. How to caress a woman. A man in control. The type of man she had vowed to avoid from now on. She needed to be in control.

Still, she itched to get beneath his skin and find out his secrets. After his confrontation with the detective, she had witnessed his anger. Later she'd seen sadness in his dark eyes. Despite his tough facade, she sensed his compassion. Not many men would provide a service to a women's shelter without garnering any profit for their fledgling company. She wondered if he had some other motivating force. She wanted to find out.

She'd call him tomorrow. Maybe even apologize for her reckless behavior. Truth was, she wasn't at all sorry. And if she had it to do all over again, she wouldn't change a thing. That was a dangerous concept. She could stand to lose a lot, namely her heart.

No, she wouldn't allow that. If anything happened between her and Zach Miller, it wouldn't go beyond the physical. She did want him, she couldn't deny that. And apparently he wanted her, too. So what was wrong with indulging in a little physical gratification? They were both consenting adults. And it had been a very long time.

Then something occurred to her. What if Zach withdrew his offer because of what was happening between them? He didn't look too pleased when she'd left him alone with Gil. Surely he wouldn't. But how could she be certain?

She couldn't wait until morning to make the call. She would never get any sleep unless she knew things were okay between them and she hadn't compromised her plans for the shelter.

Glancing at the clock, she realized it was nearing midnight. But Zach had said he was a night person. If her hunch was correct, he was probably still up.

Midnight came and Zach was still up, in many respects. He'd downed his second cup of coffee in the comfort of his well-worn leather lounger and was starting on his third.

The monotonous tick of the clock broke the silence in his apartment. He considered turning on the stereo and immersing himself in the mournful sounds of a saxophone. But he wasn't in the mood for music. What he was in the mood for required a more hands-on approach.

Yeah, thanks to Erin Brailey he couldn't fall asleep even if his mental health depended on it. Luckily he didn't require much rest. He had a feeling he wasn't going to get much in the nights to come unless he made a conscious effort to get her out of his system. What that entailed he had no idea.

The shrill of the phone brought him out of his musings.

Damn. All he needed right now was some kind of security crisis that his men couldn't handle. Then again, maybe that's exactly what he needed. Something to get his mind off Erin.

He reached for the cordless phone on the end table and answered with his pat, ''Miller here.''

''Were you asleep?''

The sultry sound of her voice brought every part of him to attention. He pulled the lounger upright, almost tipping the coffee into his lap. Maybe that wasn't such a bad idea. ''Erin?''

''Yes, it's me. I'm sorry to bother you so late, but I couldn't sleep.''

''Yeah? Me, neither,'' he admitted, although he wasn't sure why. But for some reason he couldn't imagine being anything but honest with Erin from now on. Which meant someday soon he'd have to tell her the truth about Andrews. But not tonight.

''I wanted to tell you I appreciate the work you're doing with the shelter,'' she continued. ''I also wanted to say I enjoyed this evening.''

When the thought of Erin's kisses filtered into his brain, he set the coffee cup down on the table. If he didn't, he'd be in danger of garnering third-degree burns on his bare chest or another strategic area. ''Could've fooled me, the way you hightailed it out of there.''

''I know. I guess I should apologize for leaving you alone to deal with Gil. Did he suspect anything?''

''Everything.''

Her laugh was warm, sexy. ''He's a good friend. He'll probably just let it go.''

Not anytime soon, Zach thought, but decided not to

mention that. "I'm the one who should be apologizing. I didn't mean for things to get so out of hand."

"I'm not sorry at all."

He tightened his grip on the receiver. "You're not?"

"No. Does that surprise you?"

Hell, yeah. She was full of surprises. "The last thing I wanted was to embarrass you in front of your colleague."

"I'm not worried about Gil. I just didn't want you to think this sort of thing happens to me all the time."

That thought pleased him. "How often has it happened?"

"Never."

Now he was doubly pleased. "I'm glad."

Her soft sigh floated through the line. "This thing between us could really complicate matters, Zach."

"Only if we let it."

"We still have a business arrangement, don't we?"

So now he knew why she had called. To make sure everything was okay with the shelter. He understood and admired her concern. He just hoped that wasn't her only motivation. "Sure. Nothing's changed with my plans for the shelter. And as far as our business dealings are concerned, we can differentiate between business and pleasure."

"That could be hard to do."

If she kept talking to him in that breathless way of hers, he'd be facing a long, hard night. "Let's take it one day at a time for now. Get to know each other better."

"Then whatever happens, happens. Right?" She spoke as though she already knew what would happen. Then so did he.

He thought about the conference room, and he realized how hard it would be to keep his hands off her. "Yeah. I think that's a good idea."

"Speaking of getting to know each other, have you ever…" She hesitated. "Never mind."

He was more than curious. "Ever what, Erin? Like I told you before, it's best to just say what's on your mind."

A long silence followed, then she asked, "Have you ever indulged in a safe fantasy?"

That got his attention. Every inch of him. "How do you mean?"

"Talk about fantasies. Over the phone."

He swallowed hard. "No. Have you?"

"No, but I've always wanted to. The phone allows you a certain amount of freedom to express yourself. Let go of inhibitions. Don't you agree?"

"I've never thought about it before, but I guess you're right." He'd never had phone sex before, either, if that's what she was proposing. But no one would ever accuse him of not being willing to try something at least once. "I'm game."

"Out of curiosity, what are you wearing?"

He bolted out of the chair and knocked his knee on the coffee table. Even the shooting pain didn't hinder the impact of her question. "You want details?"

"Yes. I'm trying to picture you. Where are you?"

He paced back and forth in front of the sofa. "I'm standing in my living room wearing boxers. Dark blue. That's all."

"Really?" She sounded disappointed.

"They come off when I go to bed."

Another long pause suspended the conversation. Although he was wading through treacherous waters, he couldn't let her off the hook. "How about you? What are you wearing?"

"A satin robe."

"What color?"

"Lilac."

"Underneath it?"

"Nothing at all."

Okay, he'd asked for that. "Are you in bed?"

"Right now I'm sitting on a chaise on my balcony. It's a beautiful night. Clear. Lots of stars. I can smell the gardenias below my window."

Normally he didn't give a damn about stars and flowers, but her wistful tone made him appreciate things he'd never considered before. "It's warm outside, then?"

"Too warm. It's hot, even."

"This robe you have on, is it thin?"

"Yes, but I'm still hot."

The hypnotic quality of her voice generated its own brand of heat, a searing warmth that seeped through every pore of his body. "Can anyone see you?"

"Not as long as I'm lying down. The balcony's hidden by a privacy wall."

The picture of Erin stretched out on a chaise, naked, burned into his brain as clearly as if he were there. Although the game they now played was dangerously seductive, and the stakes were high, he chose to be a willing participant. And up the ante. "Then maybe you should take the robe off, Erin."

"Maybe I will."

Zach held his breath as silence filled the line. His imagination jumped into high gear. He pictured her undoing the robe, slipping it from her slender shoulders just as he'd wanted to slip her dress off earlier that evening. He stood stock-still and willed himself to ignore the building pressure in his groin.

"This is much better," she finally said.

He released his breath, but the muscles in his gut remained clenched. "Did you take it off?"

"Yes. Very liberating. You should try it."

He rubbed a hand down his bare chest, imagining her touch. "I don't have a balcony."

"Maybe someday you could share mine."

A welcome proposition. "How about tonight?"

"Now, now," she scolded. "If you come here tonight, that would make this real, not a fantasy."

He released a frustrated sigh. "What's wrong with that?"

"We agreed to get to know each other. I think that right now we should play it safe. Are you still wearing your boxers?"

"Yeah." And they were growing tighter by the minute.

"Well, I'm feeling a little self-conscious since you're still dressed and I'm not."

"What do you propose I do about that?"

"Why don't you take them off?"

He knew the answer before he'd asked the question. He just wanted to hear her say it.

He strolled into the bedroom where muted light filtered in from a three-quarter moon. Tucking the phone between his jaw and shoulder, he slipped his thumbs in the waistband of his shorts. *Gil's right, Miller. You're playing with fire.*

What the heck. He did need to get ready for bed. And he could at least be more comfortable, if that were possible.

After a moment's hesitation, he snaked his shorts down his hips and stepped out of them. He was free, hard and aching to do something about his predicament.

"Zach? Did you do it?"

He sat on the edge of the bed. "Yeah, I did it."

"Where are you?"

"On my bed."

"How big is it?"

"How big is what?" Damn, he sounded like an idiot.

She laughed. "The bed."

"King-size. And firm."

"That sounds tempting."

He wanted to groan. "I meant the mattress."

"But of course that's what I meant," she said in an amused voice. "Are you lying down?"

"No. I'm sitting on the end of the bed."

"Aren't you uncomfortable?"

Hell, yeah. This was sheer torture. Worse than torture. "I'm okay," he lied. "Thanks for your concern."

"You're welcome. I wouldn't want you to be anything but totally relaxed."

This time he did groan. "You really think I'd be able to relax thinking about you naked on your balcony?"

"I'm thinking about you, too. Imagining you."

God, he ached to be with her. Touch her. Make love to her. She was bold and uninhibited, sensual beyond belief. Something he more than appreciated. "Let's just say I did come to your balcony one of these days. What would we do?"

"Details?"

"Hey, this is your fantasy. You make it as detailed as you want." And he hoped to God he survived it.

"First, we'd have wine, I think. A nice, cool white. Chardonnay from my father's private reserve. Then we'd dance for a while to your favorite jazz. After that, you'd kiss me, just like you did today."

"What else?" he asked, totally caught up in the imaginary scenario.

"I don't know. What do you think will happen next?"

In his mind's eye he was way past the point of a kiss. But he could back up and tell her, step by step, exactly what he would do. "First you'll be wearing that same dress you had on today. I'll unzip it real slow, because it's made to be taken off that way. You're wearing a lace bra. It comes open with one easy move. Then once that's off, along with everything else, and you're standing there, naked, I'll touch you, first with my hands, then my mouth."

"Where?" She sounded winded, excited.

"Everywhere."

He heard the catch of her breath before she spoke. "But I'd have to undress you, too. I'd start with your shirt, the soft chambray one you wore the first time I met you," she said. "Of course, I'm not as patient as you. I won't bother with buttons, I'll just rip it apart. Now your jeans, I'll take them off slowly and only partway."

He had no trouble picturing it, and his body paid the price. "Then what?"

"I'd touch you."

Zach's pulse accelerated and his body screamed for release. "Where exactly would your hands be, Erin?"

"Where would you like them to be?"

His whole body lurched in answer to her question.

Zach shifted on the bed, winding tighter and tighter with every seductive word. He had to stop the game now, before he couldn't. Before he drove to her place and turned a little fantasy into reality. If she wanted safe for now, he'd honor that. Some things were just worth the wait. "Erin, we better end this. If we don't, I'm heading over there."

She released a ragged breath. "Yes, I think you're right. Will you be coming by the center tomorrow?"

"I don't know. I haven't checked my schedule." So much for honesty. He knew he was free tomorrow because he'd told his secretary to mark him out. And he knew exactly where he'd be.

"Well, if you get a chance, stop by the offices. I'll have your copy of the contract."

It was amazing how she'd turned on the professional mode as smoothly as turning the on/off button on a radio. "Sure, I'll try."

"Good. And Zach…"

"Yeah."

"Someday soon I do want to show you my balcony."

Even though the line went dead, Zach's body was still alive. Tossing the phone aside, he stretched out on his back across the bed and considered his options. He could make a call and probably find someone to rid him of his physical need. That prospect held no appeal. He only wanted one woman, and that woman wasn't willing. Not tonight, anyway.

He might as well face it. Erin Brailey was getting to him. He wanted her with a desire beyond anything he'd ever experienced. He wanted to know everything about her, all her fantasies. He wanted to fulfill them all. But it was more than that. Not only was he drawn to her sensuality, but to her strength. She didn't appear to be afraid of anything. She knew what she wanted. Unlike him.

He had no idea what he was looking for. He didn't trust himself enough to make a commitment. Especially to someone like Erin, a compassionate woman who probably needed more than he could ever give her. Most of all, love. He'd grown up in the shadow of hate and learned the meaning of cruelty at an early age. He'd also seen what love had done to his mother, driven her to an early grave from cardiac arrest. She'd survived the wounds her husband had inflicted, but she hadn't survived the broken heart.

No, the environment he'd grown up in wasn't conducive to loving emotions. Thanks to his father.

For that reason alone, he shouldn't get involved with Erin, no matter how tempting the prospect. Yet he didn't believe for a minute that one taste of her would ever be enough. But one thing he knew to be true. If he finally slept tonight, his dreams would be filled with her.

Four

"**I** can't believe this." Erin tossed the newspaper onto the blue-striped sofa and paced the length of Rainbow House's children's room like a caged animal. She skirted a pile of toys she'd been sorting through before Ann Vela, the shelter's daytime social worker, brought her the bad tidings.

"Calm down, Erin," Ann said. "It's just a letter to the editor. It's not so terrible."

"It's terrible enough." Erin snatched up the paper again and silently cursed Ron Andrews. "He says here, 'The Rainbow Center has decided to stick its nose where it doesn't belong by opening a place for cops' wives to run to after a family dispute. I say it's none of their business.'" Erin rolled her eyes. "A place to run to after a family dispute. Jeez, this man's a Neanderthal. He makes it sound as though the shelter's only for policemen's wives. He conveniently fails to mention it will house other high-risk residents.''

Erin looked up to meet Ann's kind eyes. The counselor had an uncanny way of soothing frazzled nerves, a talent that made her invaluable to the shelter's residents. And Erin, too. But it would take more than Ann's tranquil demeanor to ease Erin's current distress.

"What are you going to do about it?" Ann asked.

Erin cast another glance at the paper as she walked past the sofa again. "He took some pretty serious potshots at Phase II. I'll probably get in touch with a reporter from the paper and see if she'll do a story now that the news is out."

"Good plan." Ann folded an arm across her waist and tapped her chin with one fingertip.

Erin recognized her thinking mode. She also recognized Ann's concern. "What's wrong?"

"This Andrews fellow, what do you know about him?"

Erin shrugged. "Not much."

"Do you think there's more behind this verbal bashing than his concern about PR for the department?"

Erin paused and rested her hands on the back of the sofa. "What do you think?"

Ann's smile was cynical, knowing. "I wouldn't be surprised to learn he roughs up his wife every night after he goes home."

"Could be. Then again maybe we're reading more into it because we don't like what he's done."

Yet the moment Erin had read Andrews's letter on the editorial page, she'd wondered that very same thing. And she had a feeling Zach Miller might be able to answer her questions. If she could get him to come clean.

Pleasant chills swept over Erin when she thought about Zach. It wasn't the first time he'd been on her mind today.

She'd barely been able to concentrate on the staff meeting that morning. She had tried to sort through some of the children's toys before school was out, but she kept putting those to be discarded in the wrong pile. He was playing havoc with her mind, just as he had played havoc with her body the evening before.

A wicked smile crept in when she thought about their phone conversation. She'd shaken him up, all right. But he'd gone along with her. And she got the distinct feeling he'd liked it. She wasn't prone to having phone conversations with sexual overtones. She had Zach Miller to thank for her sudden loss of inhibitions.

Ann waved a hand in front of Erin's eyes. "You in there?"

Erin's face heated. "Yeah, just thinking."

Ann sent her a Cheshire cat smile. "Are you having daydreams about night things?"

Erin returned Ann's smile. "I'm plotting." She didn't dare reveal that her introspection had to do with night things, although Ann would be pleased. The woman was determined that Erin "find a man." She'd found one, all right. One that was probably all wrong for her.

Several excuses to call Zach filtered into Erin's brain. No, she would let him make the next move. For now.

Glancing at her watch, Erin noticed she had less than an hour before she needed to return to the new shelter. "I better get back to work here."

"Erin." Ann nodded toward the doorway leading to the shelter's kitchen where a little girl stood.

The child was waif-like and pale, her stick legs and knobby knees exposed by the faded pink shorts. Her thin hair hung down in fine strands, almost covering her face. A hint of sadness dimmed the bright-blue depths of her innocent eyes.

Erin held out her hand, deciding she wasn't in such a hurry after all. "Hey, Abby. Do you want to finish our book?"

The child nodded. "'Kay."

Ann strolled to the staircase leading to the upper floors and her office. She turned to Erin and gestured toward Abby. "You really need to get you one of those."

Erin sighed at her friend's persistence. Her work was meaningful enough. "Give it up, Ann."

Ann grinned. "We'll just see if that old biological clock doesn't start counting down once you turn thirty next year." She headed up the stairs before Erin could respond.

Erin mentally scoffed at Ann's words, picked up the picture-book from the coffee table and sat down on the sofa. She patted the cushion next to her. "Come here, sweetie, and we'll see what the *Cat in the Hat* is up to now."

"Abby?" a voice called from the kitchen.

The little girl stopped in midstride and turned. Nancy Guthrie shuffled into the room favoring her left leg. With her hair pulled back in a low ponytail, Nancy's face looked as gaunt as her daughter's. The fist-sized bruise on her jaw had faded to an ugly green-streaked-yellow. Erin thought it looked much better than it had a week ago. Nancy had traveled to the shelter from two hundred miles away with only the clothes on her back and a frightened little girl.

"Hi, Nancy," Erin said. "How did the job interview go?"

Nancy's gaze darted about as if she were afraid to look Erin in the eye. She clasped and unclasped her hands. "Okay, I guess. I'll know something tomorrow."

"I'm sure you did fine. We'll keep our fingers crossed."

"Thank you," Nancy said, then took Abby by the hand.

"You come into the kitchen with me, munchkin. We'll fix some lunch."

Abby sent Erin a pleading look. Erin held up the book. "I'll watch her for a while. We were about to get to the good part before she left for school this morning."

Nancy finally raised her eyes to Erin. "Are you sure?"

Erin smiled. "I'm sure. She'll be fine."

"Okay, then." Nancy bent and brushed a kiss across her daughter's cheek. "Be good, Abby."

Erin couldn't imagine Abby being anything but good. Since she'd come to the shelter, the child had rarely spoken, but then, neither had her mother. Erin could only imagine the hell they'd been through. The bruises on Nancy's body served as evidence of the cruelty they'd endured, but Erin worried more about the internal scars buried deep within mother and child.

Erin sighed. She had lived a Pollyanna existence with two parents who'd loved her and provided all the material things she could ever want. Maybe her father loved her too much at times, but he had never been abusive. He'd never even threatened to spank her. She had grown up safe, without a care in the world. If only she could do more to help this child feel safe.

Abby made her way to the couch and scooted onto the cushion, a comfortable distance from Erin. Erin opened the book and tilted the pages so Abby could see, careful not to invade Abby's personal space. Trust was something Abby would have to deal with on her own, without any coercion.

Erin began to read, and little by little Abby moved closer. Midway through the second page, the buzzer sounded, indicating they had a visitor. But before Erin could get up to answer, Ann came bounding down the stairs calling, "I'll get it."

Erin looked back at Abby and noted a hint of fear in her eyes. "It's okay, sweetie. Probably just Mrs. Walker coming in to volunteer. You remember her, don't you?"

Abby slid over and leaned against Erin's side. Her heart ached for the little girl who had been robbed of her security.

Before she continued reading, Erin brushed away a silky tendril of hair from Abby's forehead. Someday she would like to have a little girl like Abby. With one exception. She'd want to see joy in her own daughter's eyes, not fear and oppression. And suddenly she felt a sudden surge of protectiveness for Abby, for all children.

If only she could do more.

"What can I do for you?"

Zach was greeted at the door by a stout olive-skinned woman with an attitude that shouted pit bull. She eyed him up and down like he was an escaped con.

He cleared his throat and disregarded her stern expression. "I'm looking for Erin Brailey. Is she here?"

"Maybe. Who are you?"

"I'm in charge of security for Phase II."

The woman frowned. "Do you have a name?"

"Zach. Zach Miller."

"ID, please."

He hadn't been through this much interrogation since he'd left the force. He flinched at the memories as he removed his wallet and pulled out a business card. For good measure he pulled out his driver's license, too. The woman took the items from him and studied them for a moment before handing them back.

She stared at him with distrust. "Is she expecting you?"

"Not exactly. But she knows who I am."

"All right," she said, sounding resigned to the fact that

he wasn't going to go away. She opened the door, and when he stepped over the threshold, she told him. "Stay in the foyer. I'll get her."

He watched the warden walk into an adjoining living area. At the sound of Erin's voice, he moved to one side of the entry to get a better view.

Erin sat on a faded-blue sofa with a wisp of a child huddled at her side and an open book in her lap. She was dressed in a long, flowing rose-colored skirt covered by a modest knit blouse. She wore flat sandals. The picture of motherhood.

Regret weighted Zach's heart when he thought of his own mother. She had read to him often, or as often as she'd been able to. Mostly on those nights when his dad had been called in to the hospital and the house had been quiet. No sounds of slaps or punches, or his mother's pleading and muffled tears. Those had been good times, but too few and far between.

Erin rose from the couch and handed the child the book. Before she moved away, she touched the girl's face with a maternal reverence.

Zach shook his head. The woman was truly an enigma. A chameleon. Not only was he surprised to see this side of Erin Brailey, he was definitely intrigued. Obviously Erin Brailey had a weakness for kids the size of the Grand Canyon. Not that he doubted she was a compassionate person. Anyone who did what she did for a living would have to be.

Zach stepped back when Erin started toward the entry, but not before their eyes met and she smiled. As her footsteps neared, Zach's pulse accelerated. No matter how much he tried to deny it, just seeing her again caused excitement to whip through him like a high-speed chase.

"Good afternoon," she said. "How did you find us?"

"I stopped by the center, and Cathy gave me directions."

Erin raised a brow. "Oh, she did, did she? I guess you just turned on the charm, and she spilled her guts."

Zach thought he detected a touch of jealousy in Erin's tone, but decided it was just his imagination. "Actually, I walked in and asked her. I was there two minutes tops."

Erin's luminous smile caused Zach's heart to leap into his throat. "Guess I'll go easy on her since she did meet you the other day."

He glanced around the area. "How many people does this place house?"

"About twenty residents. Sometimes it's not big enough." The despair in her tone reaffirmed her commitment to the cause.

Zach's admiration for Erin increased. She was a direct contrast to the women whom she helped on a daily basis. His mother had been helpless, and at times he had hated her for not being stronger.

"You haven't told me why you're here," Erin said.

He opted for a partial version of the truth. "You said I could pick up the contract."

Her face colored to a light shade of pink. "I did, didn't I? I left it at the center. Can you come back tomorrow?"

"Sure. But while I'm here, I did want to ask you a few questions about the system." If he could remember them.

She checked her watch. "I don't have much time. I was about to change clothes and go to the new place."

"This won't take too long."

Erin looked over her shoulder toward the living room, then regarded him again. "Tell you what, this isn't exactly a welcome place for a man. The female residents get nervous if they hear a male voice. When you're free this afternoon, why don't you join me at the other shelter? That is, if your offer still stands about helping me paint. We can talk then.''

Spending time alone with Erin seemed inadvisable. But Zach vowed he would remain in control even if he had to take a cold shower. "Sure. I'll go home and change and meet you in an hour."

Her smiled deepened and traveled all the way to her blue eyes. "Good. I'm looking forward to it."

Zach made record time on the drive to Phase II. He arrived at the shelter in forty-five minutes, afraid he might have beaten Erin there in his haste to see her again. But his worry was allayed when he noted a small convertible parked in the drive. Although he hadn't seen her vehicle, he knew it belonged to her. He'd often found that people expressed themselves with the cars they drove. Candy-apple-red and sporty suited Erin.

Zach bolted from the truck and willed his steps to slow so he didn't look overanxious. For God's sake, he was acting like a kid on his first date. He'd come here to help out with the project, not help himself to Erin. She was right. This could get complicated.

With that in mind, he drew a deep breath and opened the door to the house. He did a quick search of the bottom floor and when he didn't find her, he headed up the stairs. "Erin?"

"I'm up here. In the rabbit room."

He should have known he would find her there, her fondness for that particular place apparent from the first time he'd been there. Once he arrived in the room, he expected to see her decked out in old jeans and T-shirt, covered in paint from head to toe. But as usual, she surprised him.

With her profile to him, she stood balanced on the top

rung of the ladder applying some more of the bunny border to the wall. Instead of the presumed jeans and tee, she wore short coveralls and a sleeveless blouse. Her hair was piled up and secured with a plastic clip, a few strands of gold dangling at her ears and nape. She looked sexy as hell.

He stood in the door, paralyzed by the view. He took in the sight of her full breasts, her well-toned arms, her shapely calves, and immediately felt a jab of desire. He *was* acting like a kid on his first date.

"You look like a pro," he said. And a fantasy, he thought.

She turned her head toward him and smiled. "Hardly. A pro would probably tear this down and start over."

Zach recalled their conversation the night before, and the image of Erin naked on her balcony. He fisted his hands in his pockets in an attempt to hide his sins in case his body wouldn't obey his brain. Approaching the ladder, he surveyed her work instead of her. "Looks pretty good to me."

She climbed down two rungs, turned to the side and braced her shapely hip against the ladder. "It's a little crooked."

Zach looked at the border again. "No, I think it's fine."

"Okay, if you say so." She climbed down the rest of the rungs and walked to a large sheet of wallpaper laid out on the floor. Instead of kneeling down, she bent over to pick up the panel. And it was all Zach could do not to moan. The coveralls rode up, flashing the back side of her thigh.

Hell, he was insane. Certifiable. How could he spend the next few weeks trying to keep his hands to himself while they got to know each other better? Maybe with time the sight of her would grow old, like eating the same cereal every morning.

Yeah, right. He couldn't imagine ever getting tired of looking at her or being with her. That thought gave him pause.

"Can you help me with this?" she asked.

"Sure. What do you want me to do?"

"Help me hold it up against the wall. I'm trying to decide which side I want covered. We only have enough for one wall."

He took one side of the panel, she took the other, and they held it against the west wall. She braced one hand in the middle of the paper and stepped back while Zach held up the top.

Her gaze roved over the yellow floral pattern. "Hmm. What do you think?" She nailed him with her blue eyes.

I think I'd like to do things with you that I've never done with any woman. Tell you things I've never told any woman.

"I can't really tell from this angle."

"Then let me hold it up and you tell me what you think."

He blew out a frustrated sigh. "Erin, I really don't know a lot about wallpaper."

"And I do?" Her frown melted into a smile. "Just walk over there and tell me if it looks okay on this wall. Then you can hold it up and I'll do the same."

Deciding not to argue, Zach dropped his hand from the paper and walked to the door. He turned around and stopped cold. Her back was to him, arms stretched above her head as she held the panel in place. Her shorts rode up, exposing more of her thighs, sending Zach's imagination into maximum overdrive.

"Well?" she asked with a quick glance back at him.

"Looks great."

"Are you sure?"

"I've never been more sure of anything in my life."

"Then we'll put it here."

"Don't you want to look at it?"

"No. I trust you."

Baby, that's the last thing you should do.

Zach hurried over and caught the paper when it began to curl. Their bodies touched, and flames leaped out to sear him, body and soul. She slipped to one side, and in silence they laid the paper out on the floor facedown.

"What now?" he asked.

"I have to wet it, then we apply it."

"Fine. Let's get busy."

They applied each panel carefully while Zach did battle with his body. Every inadvertent touch sparked his fantasies and his all-consuming need for Erin.

After they discussed surveillance cameras and guard shifts, he prodded Erin into talking about herself. She had a great sense of humor when it came to her limited domestic abilities, an intense commitment when it came to her work and a boundless compassion when she spoke of the shelter's children. He could listen to her talk for hours about anything, about nothing. He'd even laughed at her corny jokes, because she was, without a doubt, the most fascinating woman he had ever met.

After they hung the last panel, Erin turned to him and asked, "Have you seen the *Herald* today?"

"No. I usually read it at night. Why?"

She swiped at her face with the back of her hand. "Well, it seems your acquaintance, Ron Andrews, sent one scathing letter to the editor."

Zach wasn't at all sure he wanted to know the content of the letter, but he had to ask. "What does old Ron have to complain about now?"

"Phase II. He's up in arms about the presumed bad PR

for the police department because of the nature of the shelter. So he's decided to give it a little unsolicited publicity."

Zach held his emotions in check. "He's blowing off steam, that's all. He'll get over it."

Erin brushed her palms on her overalls. "I'm going to try to convince the paper to do a favorable story, complete with statistics that support the need for this new shelter."

"Sounds like a plan."

Erin smiled. "Want to help?"

No, he didn't. The last thing he needed was to stir up more trouble between him and Andrews. "What are you proposing I do?"

She brushed a lock of hair from his forehead. "Tell me what you know about Ron Andrews. On a personal level."

He wasn't up to answering that kind of question, so he opted to be vague. "He's a hothead. Brought up in the old school that a woman should know her place."

Erin's expression turned sour. "My favorite kind of guy. Bet he beats his chest before he beats his wife."

Zach's ears began to ring. "What makes you say that?"

"Just a hunch. Am I right?"

Zach held on to his last semblance of nonchalance. "Look, Erin, what Andrews does on a personal level doesn't interest me." He swallowed hard. It wasn't exactly a lie. Just a slight withholding of the truth.

Erin's expression showed distrust. "Okay, I understand. You're not interested in helping me out right now." Her tone implied she wasn't finished with the inquisition.

Zach decided distraction might be his best course in avoiding more questions about Andrews. He caught her hand and brushed her knuckles against his stubbled jaw. "I just helped you hang paper, didn't I?"

She smiled. "How thoughtless of me to forget."

Then he found himself considering something totally outlandish. "Have dinner with me tonight."

She looked down at her clothes, then back to him. "I'm a mess. It would take me a while to get cleaned up."

"It doesn't matter. The place I'm planning to take you doesn't have a dress code."

Her eyes widened in mock surprise. "Deb's Drive-In?"

"No. My place."

Erin had outgrown asthma years before, but tonight she worried she might have a latent attack. After dropping her car off at the center, she had ridden with Zach in his truck to his apartment. On the way, each bump had dropped her stomach as if she were taking a wild ride on a roller coaster. Each word he'd spoken caused her heart to vault into her throat. Despite the fact she'd agreed to come, in hopes of getting Zach to open up about Andrews, she couldn't tamp down the thrill of being alone with him and the danger that posed.

Now she sat on a wicker kitchen bar stool while Zach stood at the stove stirring a sauce he had prepared. When she'd prodded him about the ingredients, he remained cryptic and remanded her to the perch at the granite-covered island.

She surveyed her surroundings, pleasantly surprised by the well-equipped kitchen and the adjoining living/dining area. The apartment was larger than she'd expected, taste-fully furnished with an ultracontemporary white sofa, crimson striped chairs and an antique walnut armoire. An eclectic mix of old and new that spoke of good taste. But then most likely someone else had done the decorating for him. Probably a woman.

Erin ignored the sudden bite of jealousy and turned her attention back to Zach. At the moment the only sound came from the gurgling pot of boiling water. The scent of garlic rose in the air, a luscious bouquet that reminded Erin she hadn't eaten all day. In fact, she should be starving. But right now she was more interested in the view.

Zach's broad shoulders almost spanned the width of the stainless steel stove. His muscled back, outlined in detail by the thin blue T-shirt, tapered into a trim waist. When he shifted his weight, a small sliver of torn material right below the back pocket of his well-worn jeans parted. And if she looked really close, she could catch a glimpse of flesh. She imagined running her finger along that tempting place, parting it more, maybe even ripping it open...

Good heavens, she needed to stop and reassess her reasons for being here—information on Ron Andrews. Yet she had to admit she wasn't just curious about Zach's culinary expertise. The phone call the evening before had been fun, sexy and safe. A sensual prelude. Verbal foreplay.

But had she let it go too far? Was she ready to be Zach's lover? Considering the chemistry they shared, she suspected it wasn't going to be a thinking thing. More like spontaneous combustion. Still, she needed to keep her emotional bearings.

"You sure are quiet." His deep voice pierced the silence as he dropped two fistfuls of pasta into the huge pot.

"I'm just a little tired."

"Dinner won't be much longer. Maybe another fifteen minutes or so. And it's Wednesday so you only have two more days until the weekend, then you can rest up."

She tapped her nails on the countertop. A brilliant idea sparked in the reaches of her brain. "Speaking of the weekend, do you have any plans for Friday night?"

He stopped stirring the sauce and walked to the refrigerator. Opening the door, he pulled out two beers and handed her one bottle without looking directly at her. "I usually don't make plans too far in advance. I never know when I might have to cancel."

"Well, if you're not busy, I have a proposition for you."

He leaned back against the counter, legs crossed at the ankles, and took a swig of the beer. "What do you have in mind?"

"My father's throwing a party for prospective benefactors for the new shelter. The usual social thing, drinks and hors d'oeuvres."

He set his beer down and turned back to the stove. "That's not exactly my kind of scene."

"Mine either, but I'm afraid it goes with the territory."

"What would I be expected to do?"

The movement of his large hand while he toyed with the spoon fascinated Erin. She loved his hands. "Escort me and answer questions regarding security if they come up."

"I could probably work that into my schedule."

Her pulse hip-hopped, and she released the breath she'd been holding. "Good. I'll pick you up around seven."

He shot a glance over one shoulder. "You'll pick me up?"

"Yes. That's not a problem, is it, being picked up by a woman?" Erin would wager he'd been picked up by women on numerous occasions, but not necessarily in a car.

"I didn't say that. I trust you can get us there."

She slid off the bar stool and walked to the stove. Standing on tiptoe, she tried to peer over his shoulder, but to no avail. He kept sidestepping to block her view.

"No cheating." His tone was rough but teasing.

"Not fair. I deserve to know what I'm about to eat."

He grabbed a wooden spoon from a white porcelain con-

tainer filled with myriad utensils. After dipping the imple-
ment into the saucepan, he turned and held it to his lips,
then blew on it before offering it to her. "I'll let you have
one taste."

When their eyes locked, that old devil showed up in his
dark gaze again.

Erin felt a little devilish herself. Dinner could wait and
so could her questions, at least for a while. She wasn't one
to put much stock in convention and saw no reason not to
have dessert first. The cool, calm and controlled ex-cop
looked as though he might go for a little premeal distraction. There was only one way to find out.

Instead of taking the spoon, she dipped her finger in the
creamy white liquid and slowly slid it between her pursed
lips. She took her time drawing her appendage out just to
draw out the tension. His eyes followed her every move.

"Very good," she said, streaking her tongue across her
bottom lip. "I knew it would be."

He reached to the side, dipped the spoon back into the
sauce and offered her more.

She smiled. "I thought you said just one taste."

"One taste isn't always enough."

Wrapping her fingers around his wrist, Erin pulled his
hand forward and brought the spoon to her lips. She flicked
her tongue out and gathered a few drops. "You're right.
Just having this little bit makes we want more."

His gaze dropped to her mouth, then settled back on her
eyes. "How much more?"

Her attraction to him defied all logic, but she didn't want
to analyze it. Not now. "I don't want to go steady, if that's
what you're asking. I don't have time for that kind of
relationship." But somehow the words sounded false. For
the first time in a long time, the prospect of having a serious relationship didn't seem so stifling. Then she remem-

bered her flawed judgment with Warren. Getting involved with Zach would only be temporary, for both their sakes.

The sexy gleam in his eye faded, and his expression turned stern. "So you're not willing to consider anything serious?"

"Absolutely not." But was she really willing to risk it all to have so little in return? Sure. She didn't have the desire for anything heavy. She was her own person, and she wanted to stay that way, afraid of attempting anything more.

Pushing the concerns away, she reached up and cupped his shadowed jaw. "When I want something, I usually get it."

"Are you always so sure of yourself?"

"Always." It was a convenient lie. She wouldn't have gotten anywhere in life if she gave in to her insecurities. Right now she wondered if she was making a mistake. But then, she had been loved and left before, and she'd handled it fine. Sort of. Besides, this time she would do the leaving.

Erin studied Zach's strong jaw, noting the way his whisker stubble accentuated his full lips. He looked at her as though he knew some of her secrets. He spoke to her as if he wanted to know them all. She certainly wanted to know his.

He covered her hand with his and stroked her knuckles. "What do you want, Erin Brailey?"

Erin exhaled a shaky breath. "You, Zach. I want you."

Five

The spoon dropped to the ground with a noisy clatter as Zach pulled Erin into his arms and claimed her mouth. Their bodies molded together like puzzle pieces, interlocking curves and grooves. A perfect fit. The erotic dance he performed with his tongue, his teeth, his lips, sent a whitewater rush of heat coursing through Erin. She tasted a hint of beer and spice on his tongue and smelled the musky scent of his cologne, a sensual blend that caused her pulse to race and her blood to boil.

Boil. The stove. Reluctantly she pulled away. "Something's going to burn if you're not careful."

A lock of dark hair had fallen across his forehead, giving him a just-crawled-out-of-bed look. He smiled. "Too late."

She stifled a giggle. "I meant the sauce."

He let go a curse and with one arm still circled around her waist, reached back to turn off the burners. Without warning, he lifted her up and set her on the low-back wicker stool. She gasped and braced her hands on his shoulders when he slid his tongue along her ear and toyed with the clasps on her overalls.

Just do it vaulted out of her brain so sharp, so clear, she wondered if she'd verbalized it. If she hadn't, then he'd read her mind. With deft fingers he unhooked the clasps and the bib fell forward. The straps hit the granite surface behind her with a metallic clatter.

"Hope we didn't crack it," Erin said, more out of self-consciousness than the need for humor.

"Don't worry, it can take it. It's hard."

She ran her hands up his taut biceps. "How hard?"

He raised her hand and kissed her palm, his eyes never leaving hers. "Baby, you can't even imagine."

As Zach brought his lips to hers for another drugging kiss, her limbs began to feel heavy, and her lungs seemed depleted of oxygen. She briefly wondered if he'd put something in the sauce. Maybe a heavy-duty aphrodisiac. But she knew it was only the effects of Zach's suggestive words and intoxicating kisses. His overt maleness. Primal. Seductive.

Beyond all reason, she slipped open the top two buttons on her blouse, giving Zach access to her sensitive breasts, now aching for his attention. He pulled back and released the remaining buttons. A cool wisp of air drifted over her skin, causing her nipples to strain against the lace bra. Then the warmth of Zach's palms closed over her breasts, and she was lost. Totally lost.

He palmed her breasts in tandem, brushing her nipples with his thumbs. It wasn't enough. Erin wanted to feel his callused hands against her skin. Then her bra tightened and released. In one quick move he had the front closure undone and Erin drowning in a river of anticipation.

He brushed the plackets of her shirt apart, and when he stepped back, Erin's first impulse was to cover herself. But he grasped her wrists and held them to her sides, leaving her completely exposed to his eyes.

"I want to look at you," he murmured. He sought her eyes again. "You are incredible."

Erin felt a little shy under his assessment and a whole lot hot. He studied her as if she were a priceless painting. She'd never felt so special before. So beautiful. So needy.

Releasing her wrists, he cupped both breasts and continued his erotic massage. She found herself leaning back, elbows braced on the bar behind her, giving him better advantage.

Zach fondled her nipples, and she closed her eyes as she gave in to the sensual assault. But his deep voice drew her out of her pleasant stupor.

"Look at me, Erin." With effort she opened her eyes to his midnight gaze. "I want you to see what I'm doing," he said.

Like a pawn in a game of chance, she lowered her eyes and watched as he rolled her pebbled flesh between his fingertips, then squeezed gently. A storm of desire stirred low in her belly and gathered between her thighs, drenching her with liquid fire. He brought one finger to her lips, and running on instinct, she took it in her mouth. He slowly withdrew the appendage, then dampened her nipple with it.

In that moment Erin knew she would never be satisfied until she had experienced all of his mastery.

He leaned forward for another kiss, gently thrusting his tongue into her mouth in sync with his questing fingers. Then he left her lips to feather hot kisses across her collarbone and continued on to the valley between her breasts. When his mouth closed over her nipple, a sound somewhere between a moan and a whine bubbled up in Erin's throat.

He raised his head and said, "So you like that."

Oh, yes, her mind shouted, but she couldn't make the words form in her mouth. Instead she molded her hands to his scalp and pulled his head back to her, then followed his movements as he paid equal attention to her other breast. He swirled his tongue around the hard peak, and Erin moaned. And when he released her, she moaned again at the loss.

His devious half smile made her squirm. She looked away, afraid if she didn't, she might beg him to continue. He cupped her cheek and brought her face back toward him. Once he'd gained her attention, his hand drifted down her abdomen and underneath her overalls. He slipped a finger just beneath the elastic band of her panties. "Do you want more?"

She nodded mutely as her chest rose and fell in a rapid succession of panting breaths. Time seemed to suspend while she waited for what would come.

The annoying beep of a pager thrust Erin back into reality, a place she didn't care to be at the moment.

"Dammit to hell," Zach muttered as he withdrew his hand from beneath her clothes. "This better be good." He strode to the dining room table and scooped up his pager.

Another beep echoed from the vicinity of the island.

"I think it's mine," Erin said. She clasped the placket of her shirt with one hand and fished through the front pocket of the overalls with the other. She pulled out the pager and depressed the message button. "It's the shelter."

Zach raked a hand through his hair. Frustration molded his face into a stern mask. "Do they always bug you after hours?"

"Not unless it's an emergency. I need to call."

He gestured toward the phone hanging on the nearby wall. "Help yourself."

She redid her buttons and overalls, then slid off the stool. After making her way to the phone, she pounded out the shelter's private number.

"Rainbow House." Ann's voice sounded strained.

"What's up?"

"Erin. Thank God. You need to come down here right away."

Erin's chest contracted under the weight of her concern. She was accustomed to dealing with crises, but it didn't make each instance any less worrisome. "Is it bad?"

"We have a new resident, and I think there's going to be trouble with the husband."

"Did he follow the driver?"

"No, but I suspect he'll know where she is, anyway."

"Have you put the police on alert?" Dead silence. "Ann, just spill it."

"He is the police."

Erin had hoped they could avoid this situation until the new shelter opened. No such luck. Dread knocked her imagination into fifth gear. "Who is he, Ann?"

"Detective Ron Andrews."

Zach noticed the immediate change in Erin as she white-knuckled the receiver, her face set in stone.

"I'm on my way," she said, then slammed down the phone.

"Guess you need to go." He tried to mask the disappointment in his voice, but he wasn't successful.

"Yes, I do." She gripped the back of a dining room chair. "But before I go, I need to ask you another question."

"Shoot."

"What do you know about Ron Andrews's wife?"

The question slammed Zach like a fist. For a moment he considered lying again, but the truth would have to come out sooner or later. "She used to be my partner."

"They're both cops?" Erin's eyes widened. "Why didn't you tell me this before?"

"I wasn't in the mood to go into it tonight."

Erin's gaze drifted off, then she turned her serious blue eyes on Zach. "Were you two close?"

"We worked side by side for five years. That makes you pretty close."

"Then it's safe to assume you know a lot about her personal life, namely her relationship with her husband."

Zach sighed, feeling as though he was on the wrong side of an interrogation. He should have come clean in the first place. "If you're asking if I know that the bastard beats her, then yeah, I do."

She tossed the pager onto the table next to his and released a resonant sigh. "And you didn't bother to tell me?"

"I didn't think it was any of my business." He'd made it his business years ago, and it had cost him his career.

The muscles in Zach's neck ached and he needed a drink. A strong one. "How did you find out?"

She folded her arms across her chest. "Beth Andrews is at the shelter."

Beth. Another bout of burning regret pummeled his heart. "How bad is she?"

Erin walked to the far side of the dining table, creating a large gap between them, emotionally and physically. "She has two cracked ribs and a sprained wrist. Nothing that won't heal. Physically, anyway."

Zach considered the times he'd seen Beth Andrews looking as if she'd tangled with a gang member and lost.

She always had an excuse for the bruises, and she'd refused to go to the hospital. She'd also been one of the best cops he'd known, not very big in stature, but strong in her own right. And damned smart. Except when it came to her sorry excuse of a husband.

If only Zach had done more, been a little more insistent, then maybe this wouldn't have happened. But he hadn't, and she'd chosen to stay with the jerk. Now Zach's past had come back to haunt him.

His stomach roiled, and the bitter taste of acid filled his mouth. "I'm surprised she went to the shelter."

"You must know her very well."

He shoved a chair under the table. He didn't need this. He'd dealt with Ronnie's accusations one too many times. "I didn't screw her, if that's what you're implying. I only tried to help her."

"It was just an observation." Erin walked to his side, her features softening. "Help her now."

He met her gaze and saw true compassion in her eyes. "I washed my hands of this a long time ago."

She laid a gentle hand on his arm. "She's taken the first step, but Ann says she might not stay. If you could at least try to convince her—"

"She won't listen."

"You have to try."

The thought of facing Beth again was daunting. He still harbored so much anger toward her, he might do more harm than good. But if he walked away now without giving it one more shot, he couldn't live with himself.

With a frustrated growl, he shook off Erin's hand and kicked the chair. "Okay, I'll do it. But it won't work."

"Maybe not, but it's worth a try." Erin picked up her bag from the table and dropped her pager into it. "You'll have to come with me or they might not let you in."

So much for a nice quiet dinner, Zach thought. So much for a nice quiet life.

Erin didn't know what to expect of Beth Andrews, but she hadn't expected the small-framed woman huddled in the corner of Ann's sofa, one arm in a sling, her brown hair a mass of curls.

Erin hated to disturb her; she looked so peaceful in sleep. But Zach was waiting outside the counselor's office until Erin could tell Beth he was here. If Beth refused to see him, then they wouldn't force the issue. And although Ann wasn't comfortable with Zach's presence, she had finally acquiesced when Erin insisted it might be their only chance in convincing Beth to stay, at least for the night.

Erin perched on the arm of the sofa and spoke softly. "Mrs. Andrews, are you awake?"

The woman opened her right eye. The other was swollen shut, an angry blue-black bruise already making an appearance. "Yes." The word came out in a croak.

"I'm Erin Brailey, the shelter's director. Can I get you anything right now?"

"A ride home."

"Are you sure you want to do that?"

Beth touched a finger to the cut in the corner of her lip and winced. "If I don't, he'll find me eventually. That might put you in danger."

"We're not worried about that."

"You should be. He hates this place. Imagine that." Her laugh was abrupt, humorless.

Erin rose. "There's someone here to see you. He wants to talk to you, if you agree."

Beth straightened, pain and fear etched in her battered face. "Oh, God, he's already here?"

Erin laid a hand on her shoulder. "It's not your husband. It's Zach Miller."

Beth's fearful expression collapsed into one of confusion. "Zach's here?"

"Yes. He's working out the security details on our new shelter. He was with me when I got the call."

Beth leaned her head back against the sofa and stared up at the ceiling. A lone tear drifted down from the corner of her swollen eye. "Sure. Why not? What's a good tongue-lashing compared to Ron's punches?"

"He only wants to talk to you for a while. He's not here to pass judgment."

"No, I suppose he's not. He never did."

"Should I get him now?"

She nodded and swiped at her face with the back of her hand. "Okay."

Erin took one last glance at Beth and headed for the door. Once outside, she found Zach leaning against the wall, his jaw clenched tight.

"She'll see you now," Erin said.

"Is she okay?"

"As okay as can be expected."

Zach pushed off the wall and strolled to the door. With his hand on the knob, he turned back to Erin. "Do you want to join us?"

Yes, she did. But she wouldn't. "I'll give you some time alone. Call if you need me. I'll be right here."

Zach drew in a cleansing breath and opened the door. Beth sat on the sofa, a look of determination plastered across her battered face.

Damn him! he thought as his gaze roved over her. A thousand memories played out in his mind while anger ate at his soul.

She raised one eye to his; the other narrowed to a slit. "Good to see you, Zach. It's been a while."

He took slow, halting steps toward the sofa. What could he say that he hadn't said to her at least a hundred times?

Beth shifted and grabbed her side with a groan. "I know what you're thinking. She finally got the nerve to leave. And it seemed like a good idea at the time, but I can't stay here."

Zach perched on the edge of the sofa next to her. "Then why did you come?"

She lowered her eyes and plucked at the blue sling on her arm. "Some woman offered a card at the hospital. She didn't believe me when I said I'd fallen. She made the call for me."

Zach rubbed his chin. Maybe she was making some headway after all. "If you leave here, where are you planning to go?"

"To my sister's."

"Hell, Beth, she lives two blocks from you. Ronnie will look there first."

"Then I'll go home."

Fury caused Zach to bolt off the couch. "When is it going to end, Beth? When are you going to realize that son of a bitch you married is never going to stop? When he leaves you lying in some alley with a bullet in your head?"

A steady stream of tears rolled down her face and dropped from her chin. "Maybe I'd be better off dead."

Zach moved back to the couch and grasped her shoulders. "No you wouldn't. He would, but not you."

She brushed her face with the back of her hand. "I bring a lot of this on myself, you know."

Same song, fiftieth verse. "What did you do this time, Beth? Mismatch his damned socks?"

"I didn't say anything when he got passed over for the promotion. I could've at least said I was sorry."

"Were you?"

"No. I'm glad. He's getting worse. His fuse keeps getting shorter and shorter."

The understatement of the year. "You should know by now it doesn't matter with Ronnie. You can't change him."

"He got a little better after you left the department. For a while, anyway."

"That was a token effort on his part. He was worried he might get suspended if I reported him to Internal Affairs." And Zach regretted he hadn't made that report, but he'd promised Beth he wouldn't. Many a night since that time he'd spent hours wondering if he'd done the right thing by honoring her request. But the silent code that existed between police partners prevented him from going against her wishes.

Her gaze skittered away. "I don't know what to do."

"They'll take care of you here. Find you another house to stay in. I'll make sure you're safe."

The damn burst, and Beth's eyes flooded with a fresh river of tears. Zach did all he could think to do—hold her. She leaned into him, dampening his T-shirt and clutching him as if he were a lifeline. He'd never been that good at providing comfort, and he felt damned guilty about it.

Ronnie Andrews had been his friend back then. But that was before the physical beatings had begun. Once Ronnie crossed that line, their friendship had dissolved into a heap of lies and deceit.

Zach pushed the regrets aside and rubbed Beth's back. "It's going to be okay now. You've taken that first step. You just have to take it one day at a time."

She nodded against his chest. "I'll try. As long as you promise not to call the department just yet."

The same promise he'd made three years ago. "I'm not sure I want to do that."

"Then I'll go home tonight."

Zach released a resonant sigh. "Okay. I promise I won't call until I clear it with you."

The eerie sense of déjà vu put Zach's soul in a vise, tightened by a past that wouldn't die.

Erin paced the length of the hall, waiting, wondering, until she heard the rat-a-tat of footsteps.

"Everything's all set," Ann said as she rounded the corner and made her way to Erin. "Sheila's going to stay over when Jim gets here at midnight. That makes two security guards on duty until we can get Beth Andrews placed out of town somewhere."

"I hope it's enough."

"He probably wouldn't think of looking for her here. And she told me earlier that he's working a robbery in Pleasant Oaks. That should buy us time, or so she says." Ann nodded toward the closed office door. "How long has he been in there?"

"A few minutes."

"What don't you go in and tell her we have a room ready?"

Erin grabbed the excuse and ran with it. "Okay. She needs her rest, anyway. If she decides to stay."

Slipping the door open partway, Erin saw Zach holding Beth Andrews in his arms, stroking her back with one large hand. Erin braced herself against conflicting emotions, torn between an irrational feeling of envy and the inherent need to help this distressed woman.

She considered closing the door on the scene until Zach looked up. "I'm sorry to bother you."

"Come on in," he said, but didn't let Beth go.

Erin hovered over the sofa and called up her professional demeanor. "We have a bed ready now, Mrs. Andrews. You can get some rest and think things through tomorrow. Then we can see about finding another shelter or safe house out of town."

Beth lifted her face from Zach's shoulder. "What about tonight? He could come here."

"We have two guards in place, and our maintenance man lives in the cottage out back. He's been put on alert, too."

"Just for tonight," Zach said. "I'll send one of my men over, too." He looked at Erin. "If that's okay."

"I'm sure that will be fine. And I can call the department and put them on alert."

Beth's frame went rigid. "No."

Erin flinched at the terror she saw in Beth Andrews's eyes. "But they can—"

"I promised Beth we'd wait," Zach said. "Give her some time to think things through." He brought his attention back to Beth. "You can trust Erin. She wouldn't put you in jeopardy."

Beth sniffed and swiped at her battered face. "Okay, but will you stay until I fall asleep?"

Zach glanced at Erin. "Do you mind if I stay for a while?"

Feelings of hurt threatened to surface, but Erin kept all emotion from her voice. "Sure. For a while."

Zach helped Beth from the couch. "Show us where to go."

Erin opened the door to do just that, but she couldn't

stay a moment longer. "Ann will get you settled in. I'm going home to try and get some sleep."

He smiled. "I'll see you later. Thanks, Erin. For everything."

Erin masked the confusion she felt with an answering smile. "Just doing my job."

"And you do it well." His expression turned serious. "Try to get some sleep, okay?"

With his obvious concern, Zach Miller threw Erin emotionally off-kilter once again. Made her feel things she didn't want to feel. Now she doubted sleep would come.

Six

After a quick shower, Erin wrapped up in a terry robe to face what was left of the night alone. Emptiness had been her companion since she'd arrived home. She had turned to a scoop of almond fudge ice cream for comfort. Although it filled her stomach, it had done nothing for her soul.

Why had she felt so dismayed by Beth Andrews's relationship with Zach? And how could she have let personal feelings enter into the mix when it came to the care of a resident?

Knowing the questions would continue to march into her head as she battled for sleep, she opted not to go to bed. Maybe she would read awhile. Maybe she would even cry. For some reason tears burned behind her eyes. Probably just fatigue. Nothing that a cup of tea wouldn't cure.

A few moments later she walked from the kitchen into

the darkened living room carrying a medical thriller and a cup of chamomile. She fumbled for the switch on the floor lamp next to her favorite chair and snapped it on.

"Can't sleep?"

Erin's heart leaped into her throat, and she gasped. She whirled around to find Zach reclining in the club chair next to the double window.

She hurled her book at him. He raised his hands to block the missile. It landed in his lap and dropped to the floor as he vaulted from the chair.

With trembling fingers, she set the teacup down on the end table and placed a hand over her runaway heart. "You almost scared me to death!"

"I'm sorry. I wasn't thinking."

"No kidding." As her anxiety lifted, she noted his red-rimmed eyes. His mouth formed a thin line, and he looked as though his emotions had him in a headlock.

Her fear and anger began to fade. "How did you get in?"

"You need to use your dead bolt."

"Obviously. How did you know where I live?"

"I followed you."

So he hadn't stayed more than a few minutes with Beth. Maybe she'd overreacted. "Did you leave before she fell asleep?"

"No. She was out the minute her head hit the pillow." He took a few steps toward her. "You rushed out hell-for-leather without saying good-night."

"That's what telephones are for."

"I wanted this good-night to be face-to-face."

Memories of Zach's touches earlier that evening flashed in Erin's mind. She could tell by his crooked smile that he remembered, too.

No, she wouldn't go there. She had too many questions

now to just slide back into his arms. From what she'd witnessed tonight, she suspected there was more to his relationship with Beth Andrews, whether he admitted it or not.

Erin gestured toward the end table. "I'm having some tea. Do you want some?"

"Do you have any whisky to put in it?"

"I have brandy."

"That'll do. But forget the tea."

Erin wandered to the wet bar for Zach's drink. She opened the cabinet and eyed the snifters lined up like crystal soldiers on the shelf. She opted for a tumbler, filling it three-quarters full.

When she turned, he was right there, only a hair's breadth away. She offered him the glass. "Your drink, sir."

"Thanks." His dark eyes sent her pulse skittering.

She sidestepped him and headed toward her chair, and safety. Once she settled in, she motioned toward the nearby love seat. "Sit down and tell me how you managed to convince Beth to stay."

He dropped onto the sofa with a heavy sigh. "She's only agreed to stay overnight. She's not too keen on relocating." He took a long drink of the brandy. "I hope your counselor can convince her otherwise."

"Ann's great, but she's not a miracle worker. Beth has to want to leave him for good. And maybe she will, since she's never taken this big a step before."

"I won't bet on it." Zach set his drink on the coaster resting atop the oak coffee table and eyed the living room. "Pretty damned opulent for a garage apartment. Who lives in the mansion on the hill?"

"My father."

His smile came slowly. "Oh, yeah?"

She turned her attention to the marble sculpture on the table. When she graduated from college, her father had given it to her along with a lecture on how she should tailor her career so she could afford such a priceless work of art. "I know. You're thinking it's really bizarre that a woman nearing thirty still lives on her father's property—"

"Erin."

"—but I assure you I'm here because my salary is limited, and I can't afford anywhere else. Besides—"

"Erin."

"I don't actually live with him—"

Zach's mouth swooped down on hers in an insistent, seductive kiss. She hadn't even noticed he'd gotten up. Right now she didn't notice much of anything except the taste of brandy on his tongue and the way his strong hands held her face in place for his knock-me-senseless kiss.

Once they parted, he braced his hands on the armrests on either side of her. She stared up at him, momentarily too stunned to speak. "Why did you do that?"

He leaned closer. "Three reasons. Number one, you wouldn't shut up. Number two, I don't give a damn about why you live close to your father, that's your business. And three, I've been dying to kiss you since you walked in here with your hair all wet, smelling like flowers and wearing that robe."

She flipped the sash up. "This? It's terry. Old terry."

He rubbed a fingertip down her cheek. "Sweetheart, you'd look good in rags."

She opened her mouth for a rebuttal, then snapped it shut. Oh no, you don't, she thought. She wanted answers, not his kisses and compliments. She'd worked up a good deal of determination, and he was trying his best to shatter it with his sexy words and lips. She refused to let that happen.

Erin pushed his arm aside and stood, needing to create a substantial distance so they could talk. However, she doubted she could achieve that as long as he occupied the same small space. Searching for more room to roam, she turned toward the double French doors. Fresh air seemed like a good idea. She whisked out onto the balcony.

The humid night breeze ruffled her still-damp hair, and she drew in several cleansing breaths. Maybe here she could recover her emotional bearings. Here she might be safe from feelings for Zach that ran too deep to comprehend.

Erin walked to the edge of the balcony and rested her hands on the brick wall surrounding the perimeter. A gentle gust of wind brought with it the scent of gardenias and roses from the garden below. She thought about the phone call, the way his voice had caressed her while she'd lain naked underneath the star-studded sky. And earlier, when he'd done things to her that sent her senses reeling and her whole being topsy-turvy.

Now he was here, and she was afraid she wanted too much.

She heard footsteps and held her breath. The faint smell of Zach's musky cologne overrode the fragrant flowers. His unique scent was much more enticing, more erotic and inviting than twenty acres of lilacs.

"Why do you keep running away from me?"

The sound of his husky voice peppered her arms with gooseflesh, but she didn't dare turn around. Or make any stupid admissions. "I'm not…running away." Her faltering words belied her conviction.

"Do you want me to leave?"

"I want to know why you're really here."

"If you think it's only to finish what we started this evening, you're wrong." His voice was laced with anger.

She turned to face him and met his expression, cloaked in the armor of control. "Then tell me why."

His glance slid away for a moment, then came back to her. "I want to understand what's going on with Beth. I want to know why she won't leave him."

So that was it. He wanted her expertise, not her. Erin erected a fortress around her emotions and called up a professional guise. "Living with a batterer is like living in a POW camp. A woman can only be told so many times that she's no good, no one would want her, before she starts believing it."

"That's not true. She's a good woman. There are a lot of men who would want her."

Do you, Zach? Erin tucked the question away for the time being. "She doesn't believe that right now."

"But she's a good cop. Or was."

"She's no longer on the force?"

"No. She quit. She said he wanted her to get pregnant."

Erin's stomach turned at that prospect. "She's not, is she? Because if she is, there's a good chance the abuse will escalate during the pregnancy if she goes back to him."

"She's not, thank God." He slipped his hands in his back pockets and surveyed the night sky. "She says she loves him."

Was that why he was here? Because Beth Andrews still wanted her jerk of a husband and not Zach? "She probably does love him."

He looked at her, confusion calling from his dark eyes. "How? Why?"

"Love counts for only part of her reasons for staying in

this situation. It has more to do with his emotional hold on her."

He shook his head. "I don't understand any of this. How could you love someone so much that you let them beat and berate you? It doesn't make any sense."

"Abusive relationships never do to most people. Neither does love." She had come to that realization long ago.

He pulled his hands from his pockets and dropped them to his sides, fists clenched tight. "I feel so damned helpless. I wish I could do more."

"You can't rescue her from herself. All you can do is hope she'll come around. Maybe she will with your support."

"I doubt it."

"Don't sell yourself short, Zach. You can be very persuasive." How well she knew.

He inched closer to her. "Can I?"

His dark eyes spoke to something primal buried deep within Erin. Something so very powerful it made her want to escape, but she couldn't escape. What kind of hold did he have on her?

Whatever it was, she had to regain her common sense. She didn't know his true feelings for Beth Andrews. And she didn't know if he really felt anything more for her than chemistry—exactly what she'd wanted to exist between them in the first place. Then why did that thought suddenly hurt so bad?

"Zach, it's late. We both need to go to bed."

"Lead the way."

"I meant alone."

Ignoring her suggestion, Zach's gaze roved over Erin's beautiful face—her small straight nose, her full lips, her eyes still radiant even in the muted light. Her determined look enticed him. She wasn't anything like Beth, or his mother. She was strong and self-assured. Right now he needed that. He needed her.

She brushed away a golden tendril from her face. "What are you looking at?" she asked.

"A beautiful woman."

She held his gaze and laughed. A soft sexy laugh that made the muscles in his gut clench. "It's dark out here. I guess that explains your poor vision."

"Now look who's selling themselves short." He moved forward and gripped her waist, aligning his body to hers. She didn't push him away, so he took a chance and ran his fingers through her damp hair, molding her scalp.

Her lips parted, all the invitation he needed. He brought his mouth to hers. The kiss was demanding and wild, their tongues tangling and probing in a familiar ritual. He pressed her back into the wall and thrust his hips forward so she could feel how much he wanted her. But there was too much material between them. He wasn't satisfied. He wouldn't be unless he took her to bed and made love to her right now. Lose himself in her. Let her help him forget everything.

She broke the kiss. "Zach, we need to talk."

He framed her face with his hands. "I don't want to talk right now. I want to be with you."

She studied him with a questioning gaze. "Do you want me or just a little comfort?"

He wanted both, and only she could give him either. He couldn't get enough of the taste of her, the feel of her body, her resounding strength. "You, dammit. I want you. I want to be inside you. I'm dying because I want you so bad."

Clasping her bottom, he pulled her closer. She dissolved into him, soft and facile in his arms. He showered more kisses on her neck and nuzzled his nose in the valley between her breasts. "Let me make love to you," he murmured.

"Zach…"

He looked up and met her dreamy gaze. "If you don't want me, then tell me to go."

Not giving her time to respond, he loosened the sash on the robe, allowing it to fall open. For a moment he looked down and savored the sight of her full breasts, the scrap of lace barely covering her lower body.

Zach slipped his hands inside the robe, circling her bare waist. After raising his shirt, he brought her back against him. The feel of her naked breasts pressed against his bare chest drove him wild.

"Zach, this isn't a good idea," she murmured.

"No. It's a great idea." He kissed her again, softly moving his tongue between her lips, suggesting what he wanted to do to her body.

She broke the kiss but still clung to him. "Not here."

He slipped his hands down her back and cupped her bottom. "I thought you wanted to show me your balcony."

She glanced toward the well-lit house to his right. "That was the other night. I was talking out of my head. I seem to lose my control around you."

He removed one hand from beneath her robe and tipped her chin up so she could see his eyes. See how much he wanted her. "Erin, I need you. Not in just the way you think. This isn't only about sex, or chemistry. I care about you. A lot."

Suddenly she tensed. Pushing out of his arms, she stepped back and redid the robe. "If anyone is awake on the second floor, then they could see us. The wall's not that high."

"Does your father own a gun?" Zach asked, attempting

to lighten the mood. "In case he finds me here, trying to make love to his daughter in broad open spaces."

"He wouldn't shoot you."

"That's good to know."

"He has people who do that sort of thing."

Zach laughed. "Great."

She hugged her arms tightly about her waist. "He probably is awake, watching us. Meddling in my business as usual."

Zach wondered if her balcony scenario had as much to do with the desire to rebel against her father as it did an unfulfilled fantasy. "You're a grown woman, Erin. You shouldn't care what he thinks."

She turned her back and propped her arms on the wall. "I know. It's stupid. But you don't understand. He considers me his biggest..." Her voice trembled, and Zach detected tears.

He couldn't stand the thought of Erin crying. Not Erin, so strong and self-assured. Dealing with Beth's tears tonight had been bad enough.

He braced his hands on her shoulders. "Your father considers you his biggest what?"

"Failure." She said the word with anger, without even a hint of sadness.

"How's that?"

She finally turned to face him, nervously twisting the ring on her finger. "It's complicated, Zach."

"I can do complicated. I went to college before I became a cop, so I'm not as dumb as you think."

"I don't think that at all." Her smile appeared for a moment, then faded. "When I was sixteen, I went a little wild after my mom died. He sent me to an all-girl boarding school to hide me, since it was an election year. Out of sight, out of the media's mind. I got into more trouble there. I'd sneak out at night and meet up with a boy I met at the movies. I drank some, too. They finally sent me home, and I finally got his attention. He won the election, but he still won't let me forget it.''

''We've all made mistakes.'' God knew he'd made his share. ''I would think he'd be proud of you now.''

''Yeah, you'd think. But he's not. Working for the center is beneath me, in his opinion. He'd rather I run his business than do something I care about. I think that in some strange way he still feels the need to keep his eye on me. Control everything I do. Make sure I don't step out of line.''

He drew her into a hug, determined to show her how much he wanted her for who she was, even if it took all night. ''You're a big girl now, Erin. You shouldn't care what he thinks. You know what I think? I think you're an incredible woman, and your father's a fool not to see it. I wish I knew what to say to convince you how much I care about you.''

Again her frame went taut. ''This thing between us is happening too fast, Zach. I'm afraid...''

''Afraid of what?''

''Nothing. I just need some sleep.''

In a matter of minutes she'd raised an emotional wall that Zach was just now beginning to understand. ''Erin, I'm afraid, too. I'm not good at relationships. But I'd be willing to try if you—''

''Don't say anything else.'' She stepped out of his arms. ''It's late. I think you'd better go.''

Anger bit into him, not because she was leaving him physically unsatisfied. He could deal with that. Because she was shutting him out. ''So that's it, huh? A little bit of wish fulfillment and then it's over?''

Her eyes widened. ''That's not true.''

Realizing if he pushed too hard, he'd drive the wedge further between them. He didn't want that. "Look, Erin, if you'll let me stay, we don't have to do anything but hold each other. Just be together tonight. I don't think either of us wants to be alone."

She lowered her eyes. "I'm sorry. I just think we can avoid problems if you're not here in the morning."

He clutched her shoulders and looked into her eyes, hoping to find some answers there. "Are you afraid Daddy won't approve of you making love with me, or just me in general?"

She looked away. "I don't know what you mean."

He grasped her chin and forced her attention back to him. "You damn well do know. You don't want his control, but you're still that little girl trying to gain his approval. So do you play this game all the time?"

She flinched, and he dropped his hand. "It's not a game, Zach."

"It sure looks that way to me." He touched her face, this time with tenderness. "To hell with your father. We're good together, Erin. And it's only the beginning."

"Look, as you said, I'm a big girl, so you can spare me the sweet words. I know what this is."

Anger bubbled up inside him. "Then you tell me what it is, because I don't understand a damn bit."

"Desire. Chemistry. Proposed sex between two consenting adults."

"You really believe that?"

"Isn't that really all you want?"

Hell, no. He did want more. But if she wasn't willing, he shouldn't waste his time. Still, he couldn't stand the thought of not seeing her again. "We don't have to decide tonight."

"I've already decided. It would be better if you go."

Right then the need to hold her lived as strong in Zach as his desire had only moments before. But the set of her jaw told him she didn't want that, either.

"Fine," he said. "I'll just borrow your bathroom, but I'm not leaving here until we talk this through. You can count on that."

Erin watched Zach walk through the doors without glancing back and almost called out to him. Tell him she'd reconsidered; she did want him to hold her all night. Make love with her all night. But she couldn't. Not if she wanted to shield her emotions. Not if she wanted to avoid more heartache. She wouldn't fool herself into thinking this was a forever relationship, no matter what he claimed. Besides, she didn't need forever. Even if she did, Zach needed someone like Beth. Someone he could protect. Someone who fit the mold of the perfect wife. Warren had taught her she'd never be that kind of woman. So had her father.

She'd learned from experts—the two men in her life— that being vulnerable never got you anywhere. Tonight Zach had torn away her defenses. It scared her too much. She wasn't ready to deal with that fear. And yet at times she would give anything to know true tenderness. To hear Zach whisper consolations the way he had with Beth. But at what price?

Although Zach Miller was willing to fulfill her fantasies, she'd stopped him because he'd reminded her what she didn't want. What she couldn't afford to let happen—lose her control. Her heart.

With sluggish steps she walked back into the apartment. The place looked neat and orderly, except for her teacup and Zach's empty tumbler sitting on the coffee table.

The bathroom door opened, cutting into the silence. Zach strode into the living room with his shirt tucked in and his hair combed neatly back into place.

Erin walked toward the sofa, unsure of what to say next. "I guess I'll see you at the Phase II tomorrow."

"You're not getting rid of me yet. Sit down, let's talk."

The phone's shrill startled Erin, causing her to glance at the wall clock—2:00 a.m. She picked up the cordless, worried something had happened at the shelter. What if Andrews had found his wife? She braced for bad news. "Hello."

At first there was only an eerie silence, then came the rasp of labored breath.

"Is Miller good, Miss Brailey?"

Seven

Erin strangled the receiver, her heart in her throat. It took everything in her to respond. "Who is this?"

The menacing laugh sent an icy shiver of apprehension up her spine. "I'm watching you. That's all you need to know."

Then the line went dead.

Zach was at her side in two strides. "If something's happened to Beth, then I need to know."

She lowered the phone to the table. "It wasn't anyone at the shelter."

"Then who was it?"

"I'm not sure." But she was. Almost dead sure. She simply wasn't sure how much she should tell Zach.

"Male or female?" Zach asked.

"Male."

"What did he say?"

"He said..." Erin hesitated, wondering how wise it

would be to reveal her caller's words to Zach. But he had a right to know. "He asked if you were good. He said he was watching me."

"It was Andrews, wasn't it?" Zach's voice brimmed with hatred, disdain.

Maybe she had been mistaken. "It could be."

"Did he call me by name?"

"Yes."

"Then it's him." Zach turned and slammed his fist against the wall, startling Erin again. "Dammit, he knows I was with you. Now I've put you in danger."

Erin laid a hand on his shoulder. "This isn't your fault. It's mine. Besides, it's his wife he wants, not me."

He faced her with a stern gaze, his dark eyes flashing anger. "He hates me, Erin, and he'll use you to get to me."

She clasped her hands together to keep them from shaking. She didn't want him to know she was truly afraid. "Then he probably knows Beth's at the shelter."

"Hell, yeah, he knows."

"But they would have called me if he'd shown up there."

Zach rubbed a hand over his nape and heaved a heavy sigh. "He's too smart for that. I know how he operates. He'll hide and watch. If he suspects I have a connection with Beth again, he'll be out for blood unless Beth goes back to him. And God help her if she does."

"Then we need to make sure that doesn't happen."

"How do you propose we do that?"

"All I know is that she listens to you." Erin folded her arms across her chest, suddenly chilled. "If only the new shelter was open."

"But it's not, and she's not safe in the existing one."

Erin knew he was right. No matter what safeguards they

put in place, because of Andrews's knowledge, Beth wouldn't be completely safe. And what Erin was about to propose would probably come as close to insanity as anything she'd ever considered.

"She can stay with me," Erin blurted out.

Zach scowled. "That's crazy. The idiot just proved he knows where you live."

Erin lowered her eyes and chewed her bottom lip. "You're right. I wasn't thinking."

"But she could stay with me."

Her head shot up. "Would she really be safe there? I mean, doesn't he know where you live?"

"Probably, but I could protect her."

"You can't watch her twenty-four hours a day."

"No, but I can have my men stand guard until we get Phase II completed or convince Beth to relocate."

He had a point. Still, Erin couldn't get past the thought of Beth living under the same roof with Zach. But she couldn't consider that right now. Those were selfish thoughts. She needed to focus on keeping Beth Andrews safe.

Erin sighed. "That's probably the best idea, if she agrees."

"And in the meantime I'm having someone patrol here, too."

"That's not necessary. My father has a security service on duty twenty-four hours."

"Then we'll notify them."

Erin's eyes widened as panic gripped her. "No, you can't do that. I'll have to explain everything to my father. He's already adamant about his disapproval where my job's concerned. He doesn't need more fuel for the fire."

Zach grasped her arms. "Listen to me, Erin. This is serious business. Andrews could try to hurt you."

She tipped up a chin in a false show of bravado. In reality, she trembled inside. "I can take care of myself. I know how to dial 911."

"Dammit, he is 911."

She had no answer for that. "Right now all we need to consider is making sure Beth is safe."

Zach released her and fished his keys from his pocket. "Okay, but you're coming with me."

Erin started toward her bedroom, needing some time alone to think things through. "I've got to get dressed. I'll meet you there."

"I'll wait."

She did an about-face, hands on hips. "I'll be okay. You go ahead and take care of Beth."

"I'll said I'll wait, just in case."

"In case of what?"

"In case he's waiting for you."

The silent shelter troubled Zach more than if Andrews had met him at the door. Zach waited at the bottom of the stairs propped up against the banister while Erin spoke with the evening intake counselor in the foyer, occasionally touching the gun tucked in his back waistband underneath his shirt.

Erin's shoulders slumped, and her eyes held a cast of weariness Zach knew all too well. Now nearing four in the morning, neither of them would get any sleep. It had been one hell of a night, good mixed with the bad, and his body felt the effects of both. Then his thoughts came back to Erin earlier in the evening, the way she felt, tasted.

Despite the fact he could drop in his tracks from mental and physical exhaustion, his body stirred at the memories. She had made him lower his guard and crept under his skin. He had too much to think about and too little time.

Erin dismissed the counselor and headed toward Zach. "Do you want me to wake her?"

He pushed off the banister. "No, I'll do it."

"I'll go with you."

Zach followed Erin up the stairs as quietly as his boots would let him. When they reached the upper floor, Erin led him to the room at the end of the hall. She cracked the door open after a brief knock. "Mrs. Andrews?"

Stepping into the room, Zach discovered Beth sitting on a threadbare chair next to the edge of the small bed, her fingers poised on the laces of her sneakers as she fumbled to get the task done.

Zach loomed over her. "What are you doing?"

Beth went back to her one-handed attempt at tying the laces. "I'm going home."

His mind raced as he tried to come up with a way to force her to stay. He could tell her about Ron's phone call but decided he'd keep that information as his trump card. She needed to decide on her own. "I've got a better idea. I want you to come to my place."

Beth's gaze snapped to his. "That's crazy."

"No, it's the best place for you. I can protect you there and when I'm not home, I'll have someone with you."

"What then, Zach? Hope Ronnie just decides I'm not worth the trouble and goes about his merry way? We both know that'll never happen."

"We'll get a protective order."

"And he'll have twenty days to stew over it and over the fact that he'll be suspended from his job."

"It's a start."

Erin stepped forward. "Mrs. Andrews—"

"It's Beth."

Erin smiled. "Okay, Beth. I think you need to consider Zach's idea. We're a couple of weeks away from opening another shelter, geared to high-risk cases. Zach's providing private security. If we can get you settled somewhere else until then—''

"I know about that shelter," Beth said. "That's pretty much what set him off this past week."

Zach caught a glimpse of guilt in Erin's expression as she spoke. "I know. Your husband came to see me about it. But he doesn't know where it is. You'd be safe there."

Beth rose with a wince, grabbing her side. "I won't be safe anywhere as long as he's alive."

Erin shot Zach a frustrated look and backed toward the door. "I'll let you two talk about it. I'll be downstairs if you need anything."

When the door closed behind Erin, Zach turned on Beth. "You can't go home. I won't let you."

Beth took a forced step. Her face showed the strain of her efforts. "You can't stop me."

Zach held her arm to steady her. "I have to. We've got to stop him this time." Time to bring out all the ammo. "He's out of control, Beth. He called Erin at home and threatened her."

Beth seemed to deflate, her knees buckling. Zach guided her back to the bed as she leaned against him for support. She dropped down onto the edge of the mattress. "What did he say?"

"That he's watching her." Zach wasn't sure how to tell her everything without revealing too much. Then again Beth would realize he was lying if he didn't tell the honest to God truth. "He saw Erin and me together. He mentioned me by name."

"Here?" Beth's voice was high with panic.

"No. At Erin's."

Weariness set into Beth's delicate features. "It doesn't involve just me anymore, does it?"

"No, it doesn't. So will you at least come to my place for a couple of days, give Ronnie some time to cool off? Maybe then Erin can get you into counseling."

"We did that already. It lasted for about two weeks. Ronnie even bought me a German shepherd puppy. But when it chewed on his best baseball mitt, he took it to the pound. Then he kicked me a couple of times for good measure."

Zach shook his head and gritted his teeth against the curses clamoring to come out. "How did he get so out of control?"

She shrugged her frail shoulders. "I don't know, Zach. He used to be a good man. He's always been a good cop. Maybe it was just the stress of the job."

"We were all stressed, Beth."

"But you seemed to have a handle on it."

"Maybe, but sometimes I worry I'll... Never mind."

She stood and laid a gentle hand on his shoulder. "Worry about what? That you're going to be like your father? Come on, Zach. You're not like Ronnie or him. You never will be."

"I get mad like everyone else. Sometimes worse than everyone else. Just ask Erin."

Beth smiled, a cynical one. "Well, she looks like she could hold her own. And I didn't see any evidence of mistreatment. A little whisker burn, but I don't think you held her down and tortured her without her consent."

Zach thought it was good to see her smile, even if it was at his expense. "We're not here to talk about me and Erin. We're here to get you moved to my place."

She folded her arms and assumed a defiant stance. "I still think that's a bad idea. I should go home and try to keep everyone else out of this. I've dealt with him for twelve years. I can handle him."

Zach leveled a look of disbelief after he surveyed her arm and the bruises on her face. "A sprained wrist and busted ribs isn't my idea of handling anything. I intend to keep you away from him until we can get him locked up."

"I'm not sure I want him locked up. If I press charges, he'll have to turn in his gun and at the very least, work a desk job. If Internal Affairs gets involved, he could get fired."

"Maybe that's not a bad idea."

"He'll really go crazy then."

She had a point. "We'll worry about that later. Right now we're going to put a stop to this once and for all, at least where you're concerned. Are you with me?"

"Only if you promise you won't turn him in yet."

He wanted to tell her hell no, but if he could get her to his place, he'd say what she wanted to hear. Then he'd consider his options later. "Okay, I'll hold off for now. Unless he does something else to you. Or Erin. Then I'll kill him."

She stepped back and gave him a quizzing look. "What exactly is going on with you and the lady director?"

How was he supposed to answer that? He couldn't very well say, "Just animal lust, Beth." In fact, he really didn't know what existed between him and Erin. He did know he wanted her with an all-consuming need. That she had resurrected feelings he'd kept buried for so long he hadn't even acknowledged their existence. "It was just a couple of dinners, Beth. I was at her place after you went to sleep. That's when she got the call."

She scrutinized him without judgment. "That explains why you look at her the way you do. You've got it bad, don't you?"

"I don't look at her any differently than I look at you." Man, he sounded way too defensive.

"Oh, yes you do, whether you're willing to admit it or not." Beth's sigh sounded wistful. "I just hope she knows how lucky she is."

Zach walked across the room to a picture of a single red rose in a desert, "With a little nurturing, love blooms in the most desolate places," etched beneath it. "I wouldn't consider getting involved with me a lucky thing to do."

He heard footfalls behind him, then Beth's gentle voice. "You're a good man, Zach. All you need is the right woman."

But was Erin that woman? Did he really want to find out at the risk of her rejection? Could he convince her that he wanted more than just her body? Because even if he denied it to Beth, he couldn't deny it to himself. He wanted so much more.

He turned and forced himself back into the situation at hand. "It's time to go. Let's get you out of here and into a safe place."

As Zach led Beth out the door, he vowed that this time he wouldn't let Ron Andrews have the upper hand. Let him win again. He'd do whatever it took to keep Beth safe. And Erin.

It was a nice dream. Erin savored the feather touch stroking her cheek and decided she didn't want to wake up. She wanted the dream to go on forever.

"Erin."

The deep steady voice was real. Very real. She instantly recognized and reacted to the sound with a heady warmth.

Forcing her eyes open, Erin found Zach perched on the edge of the sofa she'd stretched out on only a few moments before. Or at least it seemed she'd only been there a short while. She focused on his handsome face hovering above hers. A wonderful face, one she wouldn't mind waking up to every morning. Obviously, she was still dreaming.

"How long have you been here?" she asked, her voice hoarse from sleep or lack thereof.

"Just a few minutes. Ann said you were resting your eyes."

She propped up against the arm of the black vinyl sofa. "How long have I been asleep?"

"Not long. Beth's talking to Ann. She's about ready to go. I wanted to tell you goodbye before we left."

Erin ignored the jab of envy and feigned a satisfied smile. "So, she's going to your place."

"Yeah, but I don't know how long I can keep her there."

"Hopefully long enough until the other shelter opens or we can find some transitional housing in Dallas."

Zach shook his head. "She won't leave town. Her mom lives with her sister here. She won't leave her."

Erin sat up straight. "Have you been in touch with them?"

"I called her sister a few minutes ago. They haven't seen Ron in months. I told her to be careful, in case he decides to pay them a visit. Fortunately Kim's husband is a big guy who can hold his own. He runs an auto repair shop next door to the house. He never liked Ron, anyway."

"Can't say that I blame him." Erin stretched, her muscles protesting the lack of sleep and her cramped position on the couch. "Sounds like everything's okay for now."

"Except for one thing."

"What's that?"

"Your safety."

"I'll be fine. I'll use the dead bolt."

"You could come to my place."

Erin's laugh was short and without humor. "Sure. Me, you and Beth in your apartment. Something tells me that wouldn't be incentive for Beth to stay."

"Beth likes you, Erin. So do I." He brushed a kiss across the tip of her nose.

Erin tried not to sink into the depths of his dark eyes, afraid she might never return to sanity. "You certainly are complimentary this morning."

"I'm trying to make up for last night. I shouldn't have pushed you. It's just that—"

Erin pressed a fingertip to his lips. "No regrets. The timing's off, that's all."

He opened her palm and kissed her there. "Why don't we start over? Try again. Do it better next time." He placed a kiss on her wrist. "Slower." He moved his lips to the inside bend of her elbow. "All night."

His sultry words did things to Erin in places that normally wouldn't be awake this time of morning. Then he kissed her, undemanding, leisurely and soft with only a flutter of his tongue, and everything came to life. Erin felt it down to her toes, a slow melting heat coursing through her veins and settling in intimate locales.

He broke the kiss and stood smiling down on her. "By the way, you're beautiful when you're sleeping."

Erin's face grew warm, and a tiny flicker of unwelcome emotion reared its head. "I'll see you later."

He took her hand and gave it a gentle squeeze. "You bet. And I promise you one thing, Erin."

"What's that?"

"One of these days I'm going to have all of you. The most important part." He leaned down and rested his hand above her left breast, over her pounding heart. "I want this, too."

Then he left Erin with her mind reeling from the impact

of his words. The thought that Zach had designs on her heart sent a different kind of chills rushing up her spine, those of apprehension. She couldn't afford to give up her heart.

Later that afternoon Zach kicked back in his chair and stared at the phone. Disappointed Erin hadn't been at Phase II, he'd come back to the office after loitering for an hour when he'd finished installing the last of the sensors. He considered painting a room or two, but he wasn't sure what Erin wanted. And he sure wouldn't try to second-guess her in any matter.

He felt guilty about not hurrying home to Beth, even though he knew she was in good hands with his men. When he had talked to her earlier, she claimed she'd spent most of the day sleeping and promised she wouldn't go anywhere. Yet.

Now he had to decide what to do about Ron. Beth was right; Ron had always been a good cop. But he was a lousy husband, just like Zach's father. Both were golden boys, respected in their fields, with tempers they cleverly kept in check until they got home. Then they wreaked havoc on the people who cared about them the most.

Zach's father had died from too much booze with his honor still intact, at least in the eyes of the medical community. His mother had died several years later, never knowing what it was like to experience compassion and tenderness from the man she loved with an unnatural passion. And Ronnie lived on to terrorize Beth, the best friend and partner Zach had ever known.

Zach shook off the thoughts and reached for the receiver. If he was going to keep track of Andrews, he had to know his schedule. He called the department and learned what he needed to know under the pretense that he was trying to reach him.

After he hung up, his thoughts came back to Erin. He needed to see her, if only for a while. He could ask her to join him and Beth for dinner, but he doubted she would. Besides, he needed to talk to Beth tonight alone. Make sure she stayed put until he came up with some sort of plan to handle Ron Andrews. At least he had tomorrow night with Erin.

He suspected he'd probably hear from her before then, considering what he planned to do. But he had no choice. He would post security outside her apartment whether she wanted it or not. He'd just go to the shelter in the morning and face her wrath head-on.

Eight

"**W**ould you like to tell me who the guy was, parked in the white truck at my curb last night?" With a toddler braced on one hip, Erin said the words through a tight smile.

Zach wondered if her jaw would shatter before she unclenched her teeth. "That would be Mac. Or Greg, depending on what time you went home. Greg comes on at midnight."

She untangled the little boy's fist from her hair. "I thought I told you I don't need extra security. It was just a phone call, for goodness sake."

Now it was Zach's temper that flared. "Dammit, Erin, the man's threatening you. Quit being so stubborn."

She sent him a scathing look, then nodded toward a group of toddlers watching a video nearby. "Keep your voice down, please, and watch your language."

"Sorry," he muttered. "Why didn't you answer your phone last night?"

"I was tired. I went to bed early."

"You could've called me. Let me know you were okay."

"I'm a big girl, remember? Besides, I assumed you and Beth needed time to get reacquainted."

Yes, he'd needed to get reacquainted with Beth, talk things through with her, even though he hadn't made much headway. She was still talking about going back to Ron, but she had promised him she'd wait until the weekend to decide for sure.

Erin raised her hand to cover her yawn.

"Doesn't look like you got much sleep." He hadn't, either. He'd settled Beth into the guest room and sacked out in the lounger. Not to mention he couldn't get Erin off his mind.

"I slept fine." She looked away but not before Zach caught a flash of guilt in her eyes.

"Me, neither."

"I said I slept…fine." Her voice faltered, and he knew she was lying.

"Are you through here?" he asked.

Erin placed the baby in a playpen and handed him a stuffed yellow duck that the toddler immediately tossed onto the floor. Erin bent over the playpen and handed the animal back to the boy. "Does it look like I'm through? The mothers are in a house meeting for another ten minutes."

The baby gurgled and belly laughed as he hurled the duck. Erin retrieved it again; the baby tossed it again.

Keep it up, kid. Zach was enjoying the game and the view of Erin's derriere, her black slacks drawing tight across her bottom every time she bent over the playpen.

"Are you the only one who can watch the kids?" he asked after she found a toy the child decided to keep.

She straightened and leaned back against the playpen. "I like watching the kids."

"I admire your commitment, but you look like hell."

"Thanks, Zach. You're great for my ego."

Someone should cuff his mouth shut. "I didn't mean it the way it sounded. I meant you look like you could use a nap. So could I." He winked. "Care to join me?"

She tipped her chin up and assumed a proud stance. "Why are you here, Mr. Miller?"

Zach smiled at her insolent tone. "To tell you the preliminary work's done at Phase II. And to ask if we're still on for tonight."

Confusion spread across her face. "Tonight?"

"Your dad's house? The party?"

Erin slapped her palms to her face. "Ohmigod, it's Friday. I forgot all about the damned…" She looked over her shoulder but the children playing in the area seemed oblivious to her oath. "The darned party."

"Are you begging off?"

"No…no I can't."

"Are you still going to pick me up?"

She consulted her watch. "Yes, around seven. *If* you'll drop this thing with the security."

Not likely, but he decided to hold that thought until later. "Deal. How long will this thing last?"

She looked altogether put out, either by her obligation to attend the party, or him. "Not long. As tired as I am, I can only stand so much socializing."

He took her hand. He couldn't help it. "We'll cut out early. I have other plans for you in mind."

She tugged her hand away and braced it on one hip. "A tour of the local taverns with Gil?"

He tried to ignore her sarcasm and that she didn't seem to want to touch him. Except the latter bothered him much more than her acid tone. "Why don't we keep it a surprise?" He leaned forward and whispered, "You like surprises, don't you?"

Her mouth tipped up in a reluctant smile. "That depends."

He took her hand again and rubbed her knuckles, back and forth in a slow rhythm. "You'll like this one. I promise."

Erin promised herself she'd have a good time, even if it damaged her pride to grovel for the guests. She also promised herself she'd be gracious to Beth and keep her stupid envy in check.

She had made a quick trip home and changed, noting another one of Zach's cronies parked near her drive. Obviously he had no intention of calling off his guard dogs. She would deal with that issue later.

Erin arrived at Zach's apartment forty-five minutes early with hopes that he wasn't quite ready, allowing her some time alone with Beth, time to convince her to leave Ron for good. And after she knocked on the apartment door, she realized her plan might work since Beth answered the door.

"Come on in," Beth said, wiping her hands on a kitchen towel.

Erin moved into the small entry and followed Beth into the living room. "I'm surprised Zach let you answer the door."

"That's what peepholes are for." Beth gestured toward the couch. "Have a seat. He's shaving for the second time today."

"Thanks." Erin slid onto the sofa and carefully adjusted the hem of her dress.

Beth took the chair across from her and gave her a quick once-over. "Nice outfit. Not many people can wear red."

"Red's my favorite color."

"I can't wear it. It makes me look dead." Beth tucked one brown curl behind her ear and tugged at the white oxford shirt covering her jeans. "Blue's more my shade."

"I see you found some clothes."

"This is Zach's shirt, my jeans. That's all I've got. Zach won't let me go shopping yet, and heaven forbid I should send him. No telling what he'd pick out."

"Oh, I don't know about that. He probably has good taste." Erin clasped her hands together. "Of course, I don't really know since we've just recently met."

"Really?" Beth scooted to the edge of the chair. "To hear him talk about you, I would think you'd known each other for ages."

Erin surveyed the area and focused on several sharp-shooter trophies lining the entertainment center. "Less than a week."

"Really? Seems like I've known him forever."

"So he told me." Erin's tone sounded cool, even to her own ears.

"Look, Erin," Beth began, her expression serious. "I'm here because Zach insisted I be here. If you think there's more between us, then you're wrong. We're like brother and sister. There's never been anything between us but friendship, and there never will be."

Erin felt ashamed and stupid. She'd never been the jealous type before she met Zach. "I'm sorry if I gave you the impression that I thought otherwise. I know you and Zach are the best of friends, and I'd never do anything to come between you two."

Beth's smile came naturally. "I know you wouldn't.

And if my hunches are correct, nothing I could do or say would tear him away from you.''

Erin stiffened. ''I'm not sure that's true.''

''It's true. I know him better than most people. He's got it bad for you.'' She swept her hand in an exaggerated gesture toward Erin. ''Just look at you. Any man in their right mind would want you.''

Erin released a nervous laugh and gripped the edge of the couch. ''Thanks, but I'm sure Zach has his choice of women.''

''Maybe, but it seems he's chosen you.''

Erin frowned as she wondered exactly what about her appealed to Zach. Not that she couldn't hold her own in the looks department. She'd grown up being trained to look her best, act her best, be her best. Until recently she hadn't appreciated that concept. But since signing on with the shelter, she'd garnered confidence in her job knowing what she did mattered. And she could only hope that's what appealed to Zach Miller, not her appearance. But then why should she care? After all, it was only a physical attraction that bound them together. Wasn't it?

Just then Zach stepped through the hall entry and into the living room. His shirt hung open, and she caught a glimpse of his sinewy muscle and a mat of dark hair. ''You're early.''

Erin tried to ignore Zach's broad chest and his shower-damp hair that looked sexy beyond legal limits. ''I don't go for the stereotype of women always being late for dates,'' she said with an amused glance in Beth's direction.

Erin sought Zach's eyes again and he winked. ''I bet you like to be on top, too.''

A blush crept up Beth's face. ''Miller, you are too much.''

''You know it, Bethy.'' Then he disappeared.

Erin shook her head and smiled. "He is something else, all right."

Beth's small features turned solemn again. "He's a good man, Erin. He deserves the best. He's had more than his share of hurt."

Erin wanted to ask for details but decided to wait for Zach's revelations. If they ever came. She covered her concern with another nervous smile. "I guess anyone who hurt him would have to answer to you."

"No, just their conscience. That's worse than any physical threat on earth."

Erin acknowledged Beth's words held a great deal of truth. Guilt did crazy things to a person.

Beth rose, looking pale and exhausted. Erin stood and said, "Are you okay?"

"I'm fine." Beth rubbed her reddened eyes, one sporting a blue-black smudge. "Just tired. Think I'll turn in early."

Erin touched Beth's shoulder, hoping to broach the subject of Beth's situation. "If you need to talk to someone, you can always call the shelter. Ann's available. And I'll listen. As a friend."

Beth's eyes misted, deepening their color from gray to azure. "I wouldn't know what to say except that I'm ashamed. I'm ashamed that I let him beat me. That I couldn't do anything right during twelve years of marriage."

White-hot anger surged through Erin, although she'd heard the same admissions time and again from other women in similar situations. "This isn't your fault, Beth. Ron has learned to deal with conflict through violence. You learned to deal with him by being passive. It's a terrible cycle, one you need to break. I know it's tough."

Beth looked at Erin with her heart in her eyes. "He

wasn't always like this, you know. Ronnie used to be a good husband. Never easy, exactly, but he didn't always hit me. Before the work got to him and he tried to deal with everything with a bottle of whisky, he could actually be caring at times.''

Erin wanted to reach out to Beth and help her understand life didn't have to be this way. ''Abuse comes in phases. Good times and bad. The alcohol only gives him courage. Deep down he has a lot of rage.''

''How well I know.''

Erin felt as though she'd overstepped her bounds. Beth was an intelligent woman, and she'd lived through a hell that Erin could only imagine. ''I didn't mean to sound patronizing. I just want to see you get out of this situation. Zach wants that, too.''

''I want what?''

Zach came into the room dressed in a tuxedo, quite a contrast to the usual casual attire. An incredible contrast.

Erin tore her gaze from Zach and gave Beth an understanding glance. ''I was just telling Beth we want her to get some rest tonight and try not to worry. Right?''

Beth braced her hands on the small of her back and stretched. ''Right. I'm hitting the sack, Zach. Wake me up before you leave in the morning.''

''Greg's going to be right outside if you need anything,'' he said. ''I'll lock up when we leave.''

Beth started toward the bedroom and said over one shoulder, ''If you're here in the morning.''

The click of the door closing behind Beth pierced the awkward silence filling the room.

''Are you ready?'' Zach asked.

Erin opened her mouth, but nothing came out. It took all her strength not to stare at his broad shoulders encased in impeccable black, his tanned skin warm and rich against the white shirt, his hair neatly combed, lending him an air of sophistication. He looked too gorgeous for words. Too wonderful to ignore.

Her mind turned to complete mush when she caught a whiff of his cologne, rendering her speechless. And she thought she could stay angry with him. Wrong again.

"Ready for what?" she muttered when she finally found her voice again.

His laugh rumbled low in his throat. "Ready to go the party. Unless you have something else in mind."

Erin had plenty in mind to do with him, nothing that involved socialites and mandatory brownnosing. She slapped the dangerous thoughts out of her mind. "I'm afraid duty calls."

Zach held out one large hand to her. "Well, as soon as you're through with your duty, we'll just have to see to your pleasure."

Among the dowdy, over-jeweled matrons, Erin stuck out like onyx in snow, and Zach decided she was the most beautiful creature he'd ever seen. Not everyone could get away with wearing a red satin dress, conservative in the front but cut low in the back. Yet Erin's appearance spoke of class as she carried herself with grace through the crowd.

Zach had said a few required hellos to a few familiar faces he'd recognized as soon as they'd arrived. Now he was positioned near a massive abstract sculpture in the corner of the equally massive room. A quiet, out-of-the-way place where he could sip champagne—his least favorite libation—and watch Erin in action.

He concentrated on her bare back, uncovered to the nape since she'd pulled her hair up into a mass of gold curls.

He imagined taking each pin from her hair, one by one, but not before he got a good taste of her neck.

Erin caught his eye and smiled. He smiled back, amused at the balding councilman sporting the love-struck expression as he spoke to Erin. Zach couldn't blame the guy. Erin was the kind of woman that any man with an appreciation for the female sex could fall in love with a little. As long as it remained temporary, a man might be safe in his admiration. God help the poor sap who really fell in love with her. She would probably rip his heart out and feed it to the family Dobermans. Zach didn't want to be that luckless soul. If it wasn't already too late.

Erin excused herself and approached Zach with a sultry gait. His pulse ticked out of control, and he gripped the champagne flute with sweaty palms.

"What are you doing over here all by yourself?" she asked with a brassy grin.

"Are you flirting with me, Ms. Brailey?"

Erin rimmed the edge of his glass with a long red fingernail. "Maybe."

"Then you're not mad at me anymore?"

"A little. But I'll forget about it if it helps me to convince you to donate to the cause."

"What cause might that be?"

"The shelter cause," she said with a pretend pout. "The reason why we're here."

"If you recall, I already gave at the office." Zach leaned over and whispered, "But I'm willing to give again, non-monetarily speaking."

Erin smiled and turned her back, at the same time moving closer. "You're determined to be a bad boy tonight, aren't you, Mr. Miller?"

"I'm determined to be a very good man, Ms. Brailey."

Zach braced one hand just below her waist and stroked

his thumb back and forth over the swell of her buttocks. The satin felt cool and sensuous beneath his callused palm. "What are you wearing under here?"

Erin regarded him over one shoulder, leaving them almost cheek to cheek. "Why do you ask?"

He drew in the scent of her spicy perfume and felt heat radiating from her body. "I've watched you walk all evening, and for the life of me I can't see any lines. So tell me your secret."

Erin pointed across the room. "Later. Right now you have to meet my father."

Zach grumbled. Just when he was beginning to enjoy a little spoken foreplay, Daddy Bigbucks had to show up. Had to happen sooner or later. Might as well get the introductions over with so they could get the hell out of here. He had an angry woman to soothe.

Zach took her hand. "Lead the way."

Erin tugged her hand from his and frowned. "Tonight you're a business associate, remember?"

Anger tightened his chest in a death grip. He squelched the words threatening to explode from his mouth. Obviously, she wasn't going to let him forget that he was here to play a role. Why it mattered to him, he couldn't say. But it did matter. A lot. "Fine. I'll be whatever you want me to be."

She afforded him another smile over her shoulder. "That might come in handy."

Damn her, Zach thought. She had him playing into her hands by keeping him off-kilter with everything she did, everything she said. She was a contradiction in the most serious sense. An enigma. And he couldn't get enough of her.

Robert Brailey's face went from all business to undeniable pride when Erin walked to his side. She gave him a quick hug. Zach noted Erin was nearly as tall as Robert Brailey and they shared some of the same features, especially eye color. Although Erin was lithe and Robert stocky, they carried themselves with identical pride and determination.

"I was wondering where you had wandered off to, Daughter," Robert Brailey said with only a cursory glance in Zach's direction.

Erin's smile took on the appearance of artificial innocence. "I've been mingling for money, Father. Just like you taught me."

"Good." Robert offered his hand in Zach's direction. "I'm Robert Brailey, Mr.—?"

Zach accepted the handshake and Robert Brailey's politician grip. "Miller. Zach Miller."

Erin surprised Zach by hooking her hand in the crook of his arm. "Mr. Miller's providing security for Phase II at a very reasonable rate. We're very much indebted to him."

The elder Brailey crossed one arm over his chest and rubbed his chin with his free hand. "Forgive me, but you seem very familiar. Have we met?"

Zach cleared the hitch from his throat. "Yes, several years ago. You came to speak at the Policeman's Association Banquet."

Robert snapped a finger. "You're absolutely right. You received a commendation that evening. If I recall, you saved two victims from drowning in a boating accident while you were off duty."

Erin's gaze snapped to his. "Really? I didn't know you were a hero."

Zach damned the heat rising to his face and gave a one-finger tug at his collar. "Just doing my job." He hated accolades. Always had and always would.

"A very brave thing to do," Robert said. "So you're in business for yourself now."

"Yes. Have been for about three years."

"What's your company's name?"

"ZM Security Systems."

Brailey's hand went back to his chin. "Never heard of it."

Erin rolled her eyes. "I'm sure Mr. Miller would rather socialize than discuss business."

"That's okay, Erin," Zach said.

"Erin?" Robert glanced at his daughter, then back at Zach. "Do you know each other well?"

Erin twisted her sapphire dinner ring round and round her finger. "Actually, Mr. Miller and I just met a few days ago when we went over the security details."

"Which explains why I saw your security truck parked in the drive late one night, about two days ago. Or should I say early one morning. A rather strange time to be going over business details, don't you think?"

Zach pulled at his collar with two fingers this time, cursing the damned tie and his stupidity for not removing the magnetized sign from his truck the night he went to Erin's. He had no choice but to try and salvage Erin's reputation, otherwise she might never speak to him again. "Listen, sir, it's not what you think. There's been some trouble at the shelter. Erin's had some threats—"

"Zach," Erin said through clenched teeth, "I don't think we need to get into that here."

"What kind of threats?" Robert asked, his brows drawn down in concern.

"Minor," Zach said. "We don't think it's serious, but I've had some men posted until we can find out who the suspect is."

Robert Brailey's face took on the semblance of stone. "Why haven't you told me about this, Erin?"

"It's okay, Father. We have it under control. There's no need for you to get upset."

Robert straightened his shoulders. "I'm not upset, simply concerned. But if this persists, I'm afraid I might have to reconsider my offer to help obtain matching funds. I refuse to have your life put in danger."

"You don't mean that," Erin said, her tone low and steady.

"I do. I don't want to see you become a martyr. In the meantime, I insist on providing extra security from my service at the apartment."

Zach stepped forward. "I've got that taken care of, sir."

Robert Brailey's face hardened even more. "I know what's best for my daughter, Mr. Miller."

Zach forced down his anger and made a conscious effort to steady his tone. "So do I. I've already got my men on it."

"And that's supposed to put my mind at ease? No offense, Mr. Miller, but I know nothing about your company or what kind of men you hire."

"Only the best."

"Or so you say—"

"Could you two just stop." Zach and Robert turned to Erin simultaneously.

Ire darkened Erin's blue eyes, and Zach realized she was probably going to unload on them both. "I am almost thirty years old, and I can take care of myself." She eyed her father with a steely gaze. "All I want from you, Father, is your promise we will continue as planned with the donations." She turned her glare on Zach. "Now if you'll both excuse me." Then she spun around and headed for parts unknown.

Nine

Zach quickly dismissed himself from Robert Brailey and went after Erin. Better to face her wrath now than later, before she had time to stew over it.

He plowed past several guests, muttering, "Excuse me," as he went, trying not to choke on overpowering perfume and cigar smoke. He caught sight of Erin rounding a corner in a maze-like hall. She disappeared through an open door, and as she tried to shut it, Zach slapped his palm against the frame. He entered and closed the door behind him.

Looking around, he realized he'd landed in a bathroom. Or at least he thought it was. He could put his entire apartment in the area and still have room to park his truck. It was ornate and ugly—red velvet towels and rugs, claw-footed tub, gold fixtures, triple vanities—reminiscent of an Old West house of ill repute he'd once seen depicted in a history book.

Erin's mouth gaped as she stood at the vanity with hands on hips, regarding him in the mirror's reflection. "Do you mind?"

Zach reached behind him and locked the door. "Yeah, I do. I don't appreciate you rushing out and leaving me with your barracuda of a father to fend for myself."

She tossed her red satin purse on the countertop and faced him with a look that could mow down an unarmed man. "And I don't appreciate you telling my father about the threats. I warned you he'd overreact. Now the whole project is probably going to be shot to hell."

Zach rubbed his nape. "No, it's not. He's only testing you, the way you test him." He locked into her eyes. "Can I ask you a question?"

"What?" she snapped.

"Do you two ever really talk? Have you ever really told him what you want from life?"

Erin looked away. "Daddy talks. I listen. I gave up on honesty a long time ago."

Zach went to her and grasped her chin, forcing her to look at him. "He's worried about you. I suspect he's scared spitless of losing you, so he puts on his tough-guy face and issues demands. But deep down he probably only wants what's best for you."

She clutched his wrist and pulled his hand away. "He wants to control me, Zach. And quite frankly I'm tired of being controlled."

"He can only control you if you allow it to happen."

"You don't know him like I do. He uses whatever means he can. Guilt, obligation. In order to get him to assist me with the funds for the shelter, I had to make a pact with him. If the project fails, then I have to go to work for him."

"Why did you promise him that?"

"Because I need his help. Besides, I'm determined to make this new shelter a success."

"Do you think he'll force you to make good on that promise if you don't succeed?"

She sighed. "Yes, he'll try. When he looks at me, he still sees that sad teenage girl who can't do anything right."

"And you're all he's got."

Erin's gaze skittered away again. "Yes, I am."

"It's a damn big burden for you to bear."

Her gaze snapped back to his. "You sound like you know from experience."

"I do." He wanted to leave it at that. Now was not the time and this was not the place to bare his soul.

"How do you know, Zach?" Erin asked. "Why don't you let me in on a few of your secrets?"

He took a step back. "Later. First, let's get out of here. I need to call and check on Beth."

"Go ahead and go. I'm not ready to leave yet." She turned back to the vanity, pulled a tube of lipstick from her purse and began applying it. "Besides, right now I'm still harboring some heavy-duty anger over you telling all to my father."

He braced one hand on the counter. "What did you expect, Erin? I'm damned if I do and damned if I don't. It was either tell him about the threats or ruin your reputation. If I remember correctly, you were the one who couldn't get rid of me fast enough the other night so your daddy didn't find me there."

She returned the tube to her purse, then slowly turned toward him. "Why are you so concerned, Zach?"

"Because I care about what happens to you."

"Can't you give me enough credit to know how to take care of myself? You're just like my father, you know."

Zach mentally recoiled at the comparison. "I'm not like him, Erin. I don't want to control you. I want to keep you safe."

"It was one phone call."

"And we have no idea what Andrews is going to do next."

"I can handle him."

"Can you, Erin?" Zach gripped her arm. When she tried to wrench it away, he held on tighter. "I'd lay money they didn't teach you self-defense in prep school."

He tightened his grip, careful not to hurt her, but he wanted to prove a point. "It's not that easy, is it? Especially when someone's not trained to thwart criminal attacks."

"Let me go." Erin's words hissed out, but something flared in her eyes as he pulled her to his chest. Desire, pure and simple. At times Zach had reacted that way after a particularly harrowing call. Only he'd never had anyone like Erin to quell his lust. Except, with Erin, it was more than feral urges. Much more.

He brought her arms around him and held them against his back, loosening the grip on her wrists. "I can't stand the thought of any man hurting you, much less that bastard, Andrews. I'd kill him if he even tried."

He released her wrists and ran his hands up her arms, resting them on her shoulders. He half expected her to move away, but she kept her arms around him and said, "Do you always get what you want, Mr. Miller?"

Zach knew that look, that tone of voice. The same tone she'd used that night on the phone. "No."

Surprisingly, she nipped his bottom lip, then soothed it with her tongue. He automatically grew hard in response. "What do you want, Erin?"

She took his hands and held them against her breasts. "I want you to touch me."

As if his mind had no control over his appendage, Zach streaked his thumbs back and forth across her breasts until her nipples puckered. "Then let's go to your place."

"Let's not." Erin yanked his jacket off his shoulders. She stared at the shoulder holster. "You're wearing a gun."

"Yeah. I do that on occasion."

She ran one long finger up the leather. "How did you get in here with it?"

"Easy. I flashed the guard my credentials. Probably didn't hurt that I was with you."

After regarding the gun again, she dropped her gaze to below his belt. "Impressive."

Hell, she wanted it now? All Zach could consider was the fact he was about to initiate Robert Brailey's gaudy boudoir with Robert Brailey's daughter if he didn't stop her.

He grabbed Erin's hand, now poised on his fly. "Your place, Erin."

"No." She tilted her chin up in determination.

To Zach she looked sexy as hell, all feminine fire. "Aren't you afraid your father might discover us making love in his bathroom?"

She wrenched from his grasp and began slipping the buttons on his shirt. "He'd never think to come looking for me here. Besides, I really don't care."

Zach had to admit she was probably right, but he wasn't willing to take the chance. Or he wasn't until she traced her lips on a path down his chest, stopping to lave his nipple, then headed toward a point of no return.

"Erin…" His words slipped out on a groan as she moved her mouth lower and lower. Every coherent thought fled his brain. He tangled his hands in her hair, willing himself to pull her up before it was too late. She met his lips in a searing kiss.

Zach took several steps until he had her backed against one wall. Grasping the satin hem, he worked her dress up her thighs and to her waist, giving in to a savage need to take her right then. His need intensified when he realized that beneath the sheer panty hose, she wore nothing at all.

"I know your secrets," he murmured as he brushed his fingertips against the inside of her silky thighs, urging them apart.

Her eyes lit up with passion. "Not all of them," she whispered.

"I'm about to find out."

Zach played over Erin's sensitive flesh through the silk until she trembled with his touch. "Do you really want this?" he asked, needing to hear her say it.

"Yes." Her voice was a breathy whisper, and she arched against his hand. "Hurry."

"I'm trying, baby. Just hold on."

Zach reluctantly released her. He slipped the holster from his shoulder and laid it on the ground. Then he came back to her and with one smooth move, ripped the panty hose at the front seam, exposing more of her secrets.

"Are you always so industrious?" she asked, her words breathless, unsteady.

"I was a Boy Scout."

She flashed him a shaky grin. "I always wanted to be."

She locked on to his eyes as he slipped his fingertips underneath the tear in the silk, working his way through the soft mat of curls until he contacted warm moist flesh. Her eyes drifted shut and she sighed.

"Open your eyes, Erin," he said, wanting her to know it was him touching her.

She obeyed, her lids slowly opening to his demand.

"Tell me how to make it right for you," he said, fondling her with slow steady strokes.

"You are," she said on a sigh. "So right."

Zach kissed her again, feeling her lips quiver beneath his, and she made a sensual, needy sound in her throat. He broke the kiss to watch her face, needing to see the exact moment she climaxed.

She closed her eyes again and bit her lower lip. Zach watched her face, knowing she was almost there, totally at his mercy for the moment. Her lips parted as she tilted her head back against the wall, her breath now coming in rapid pants as she came nearer and nearer to completion.

Zach muffled her cry with a kiss and held on until he felt her pulse around his questing fingers. With a shudder she gave in to the release, collapsing against him with the force of it.

His chest heaved, his heart pounded as he held her. He wanted to slip her to the ground and get inside her. Here. Now. But he needed to wait for a better circumstance. Wait until he had her in a bed where he could do the lovemaking justice, not grab a quick roll on her father's bathroom floor.

She grasped his fly and tried to slip it down. He circled his arms around her slender wrist, preventing her from going any further. "Not here, Erin. I want to do this right. Someplace where I can hold you."

She suddenly tensed. He sensed she was again resurrecting the emotional stronghold he couldn't seem to fell.

Zach stepped back to study her face. She looked tousled and sexy, her hair falling down in golden strands to frame her slender face. Her eyes were bright, and he expected to see satisfaction in her expression. He didn't.

"What's wrong with making love here?" she asked.

Rebellion, pure and simple. Making love in her father's

bathroom was simply that, even if she didn't realize it consciously. He wanted her to want him for reasons other than a means to defy her father. "I thought we might trying lying down. Find a comfortable bed and stay there all night."

She quirked a thin blond brow. "That's rather boring, wouldn't you say?"

"Not necessarily." He feathered a kiss on her cheek. "And if you're ready to ditch this place and go to your apartment, I'll show you."

She frowned. "You need to get back to Beth. I have to get up early tomorrow and work at the new shelter."

Dammit, she was doing it again. Closing off her feelings. Shutting him out. He didn't intend to let her. "Beth's asleep, and I have a man there watching out for her. I'll make sure you get up in time."

"But I—"

He halted her protest with another kiss. "No arguments."

She looked away. "Are you doing this because you want me in bed, or because you want to keep an eye on me all night?"

Both, but he wouldn't admit it or she'd turn tail and run. "I can't think of anything I'd rather do more than watch you sleep, so I guess you could say I want to keep an eye on you." He stroked a fingertip down her chest to the cleft of her breasts. "Among other things."

For a moment she said nothing, just looked at him with questions in her eyes. "I have to say good-night to my father first. Then we can go back to my place."

Zach released his breath. At least she was willing to give him the chance to show her how much he cared for her. "Then let's get out of here."

"Good idea."

After they saw to righting their appearance, Zach followed Erin back into the ballroom. Erin's idea of saying goodbye to her father was nothing more than a wave and a quick exit. She rushed out the door and signaled the valet for her car. In a matter of moments they were in the drive at the front of her apartment.

Zach got out of the car and searched for one of his security vehicles, but none could be found. He followed Erin up the steps of the garage apartment and noted that the porch light wasn't burning. An eerie sense of foreboding prickled the hairs at his neck, and he grabbed her hand to stop her before she had a chance to put the key in the door.

She turned to him with a puzzled look. "What's wrong?"

"Did you leave your light on?"

She looked up at the glass globe. "Yes. I always do. It must have burned out."

Zach moved in front of her and unholstered his gun. Every ounce of his well-honed instinct told him danger lurked on the other side of the door. "Stay back," he barked out.

"Zach—"

"And be quiet."

He took several cautious steps to the threshold, keeping his hand raised to remind Erin to stay behind. As he suspected, the door creaked opened with a push. He took two steps forward and let go a curse. And he damned Ron Andrews once again.

Zach demanded Erin wait outside, but she couldn't. She stood at the threshold of the apartment, lit only by the small table lamp. Her gaze snapped around the room as the scene unfolded before her. Her living room lay in shambles—chairs overturned, drawers ransacked, collectibles askew like dead soldiers strewn over a battlefield.

Her heart thrummed in her chest, and her lungs felt depleted of oxygen. She was frozen by fear, terrified that whoever had violated her world was lying in wait for Zach.

Relief filled her when Zach walked back through the living room and gestured for her to come in.

Erin walked forward on rubber legs, and her eyes drifted to the broken music box in the corner. The carousel horse her mother had given her on her fifteenth birthday—the last birthday they'd spent together—had been shattered into barely recognizable pieces. So had her heart.

She slowly approached the keepsake and knelt down.

"Don't touch anything."

Zach's command brought her back to her feet. She stared down on the devastating destruction. "My mother gave this to me...I have to see if..."

Erin choked on the words, and hot tears burned behind her eyes. She was suddenly enveloped in strong arms and the sound of a deep, rich voice. "It's okay, baby. I'll find him."

Erin leaned into Zach, all her strength draining from her at that moment. She gave in to the tears because she was helpless to do anything but. She needed him at that moment, no matter how much it might cost her in the long run. She relished his strength. He made her feel safe.

"Hey, boss... What in the heck happened here?"

Erin pushed out of Zach's arms and turned in the direction of the voice, furiously swiping at her face. She didn't recognize the man, but she could tell by Zach's expression he did, and he wasn't happy to see him.

Zach strode to the stranger. "Where the hell have you been, Martin?"

He splayed his hands at his sides, and his face turned a

ghostly white. "I got a call from South Oaks. Possible break-in. It was the Weathers's place. I thought since they're your best customer—"

"Didn't I tell you not to leave here?"

"Yeah, but…the dispatcher said you told her that whenever they called, I'm supposed to drop everything."

Zach's fists clenched at his sides, and Erin worried he might actually belt the guy. "Not this time."

Martin lowered his eyes. "I'm sorry, Zach. I thought I was doing the right thing."

Zach released a ragged breath and relaxed his rigid stance. "Call it in." After the guard exited, Zach turned to Erin. "Someone from the force will be here in a minute. They'll take a report. I need to call and make sure Beth's okay."

Erin swiped away the residual tears and said, "What should I tell them?"

"Tell them the truth. Tell them about the phone call. But don't mention Andrews by name."

"Why not?"

"Because I'm going to handle this to make sure it's done right. He's smart. I guarantee he didn't leave a shred of evidence. But I plan to get proof."

Erin's fear increased. "Isn't that like obstructing justice or something?"

"We don't know for sure that it's Andrews yet. If anything comes up later, then it's my problem."

"This is *my* problem, Zach."

"Not anymore."

Erin spent an hour answering myriad questions delivered by a young police officer with a nice smile and a steady voice. He was so polite and caring that Erin hated lying to him. Several times she'd wanted to blurt out her suspicions, but Zach's stony expression stopped her.

After the officer assured her they would try to find the culprit and left, Erin requested Zach take her to a hotel. He convinced her to come home with him, in his truck, leaving her vehicle at the apartment so she wouldn't have to drive alone. She was too tired to fight, and admittedly afraid. Besides, her father would wonder where she was if her car wasn't in its usual spot. Not that it mattered. He would have to learn the truth sooner or later. Right now, later seemed best. She wasn't a good liar, and her father would have seen right through her. Yet tonight she'd lied very well to the young officer, or at least not told the whole truth.

Now, as they trudged down the walkway toward Zach's apartment, past the posted guard, she wondered at the wisdom of the decision of going home with him. She should have gone to the shelter. Or maybe even the main house armed with some excuse about faulty air-conditioning so as not to arouse her father's suspicions. Too late now.

Zach unlocked the door and quietly pushed it open. When he turned on the lamp and light flooded the living room, a strong sense of relief washed over Erin. Everything appeared to be in its place.

Zach left to check the bedrooms, then returned to Erin a few moments later with a flannel robe, set of sheets, a pillow, and a blanket. "Beth's still asleep, thank God."

"That's good."

He tossed the linens on the couch. "I'll sleep here. You can take my bed."

Erin sent him a questioning look. "Why?"

"So I can be on alert when I get back."

Warning bells sounded in Erin's head. "Where are you

going this time of night?'' she asked, although she already knew the answer.

Zach glanced away. "To see a man about a ransacked apartment."

"Zach, you're not—"

"Yeah, I am." He removed the gun from his holster and checked the chamber, then snapped it shut. "I'm going to call him on this and see where it goes."

Erin's fear for Zach's safety propelled her toward him. "Can't you let the police handle this?"

"Not yet."

"But he could hurt you."

"I won't let him."

Erin wished she could believe Zach held that much power. But Ron Andrews was crazed with anger, and Zach could end up on the wrong side of all that fury. She already had.

Erin touched his arm. "I can't let you go."

"You can't stop me." He clasped her arms and studied her with intense eyes. "I have to do this, Erin."

She could relate to that, but still she worried. "Where will you look for him?"

"If my hunches are correct, he still has the same habits. I'll turn on my scanner, see if I can find him."

Without thought, she slipped her arms around his waist and rested her head against his chest. "I'm afraid for you, Zach. I'm afraid something might happen to you."

His arms came around her, and he gave her a gentle squeeze. "I'll be okay."

She tilted her head back and looked up into his eyes. "I can't talk you out of this?"

"No." His sudden smile touched something deep inside her. Something she didn't want to acknowledge. "I promise I'll be careful, if you promise not to run out on me."

She faked a smile. "I'll be a good little girl and stay put till you get back. And if you keep your promise, I'll make you some burned toast and mud coffee for breakfast."

"I'd rather have you."

She tried to rein in her pounding heart. "I can do that, too. Right after breakfast."

Then his mouth covered hers. In the beginning it was a gentle kiss and then it grew deeper and more passionate. Erin knew it wouldn't take much to convince him to stay, simply a few undone buttons, a suggestive move, a sensual caress. But she also knew Zach wouldn't rest until he confronted Ron Andrews. She understood his determination, but that did nothing to stifle her fear for his safety. Still, she realized she couldn't convince him to reconsider. She wouldn't want him to pull that on her.

She broke the kiss and touched his jaw. "You'd better go now, or I might not let you leave."

He took a step back. "You're right."

Erin walked Zach to the door, but before he left she asked, "Do you have something I can sleep in?"

"Yeah, I do." His expression grew serious again, although a hint of emotion sparked in his midnight eyes. "When I get back, you can sleep in my arms."

Ten

Zach spotted the bastard immediately, yet he took the block twice before pulling his truck against the curb in front of the coffee shop. Andrews was resting against his black sedan, parked underneath a guard light, his beefy hands wrapped around a foam cup. He didn't afford a glance in Zach's direction, even when Zach left the truck and strode toward the place where Ron Andrews now stood.

Good. Zach wanted the advantage of surprise.

But it wasn't to be. When Andrews met Zach's gaze with a steely glare, Zach realized he'd been stupid to believe Andrews would let his guard down. They'd been trained to always be on the alert. Neither had forgotten that lesson.

Andrews spit toward the sidewalk, narrowly missing Zach's shoe. "Evening, Miller. You taking a trip down memory lane, or are you just coming up empty-handed in the woman department tonight?''

''I'm looking for you.''

Other than Andrews's slight weight shift, he didn't look at all affected by Zach's comment. ''Well, you found me. Now what the hell do you want?''

''I want you to leave Beth alone.''

Andrews's jaw went rigid. ''You know where she is.'' It wasn't a question.

''She's not with you, and that's all that matters. Where were you, say, around 10:00 p.m. tonight?''

Andrews crumpled the foam cup and tossed it in the street. ''That's none of your business.''

''I think it is.''

''Since when?''

''Since you broke into Erin Brailey's apartment.''

Andrews's face contorted, reminding Zach of a demented horror film villain. ''That's a damned strong accusation, Miller. If I were you, I'd keep my mouth shut unless I have proof.''

''How do you know I don't?''

For a moment Zach thought he saw alarm in Andrews's expression, but it disappeared. ''You wouldn't be here. You'd be down at headquarters filling out a report right now. You don't have a damned thing, so get the hell out of here before I cuff you for harassment.''

Zach had to laugh at that one. ''I don't think I'd do that if I were you. Not unless you want me to convince Beth to tell her story.''

''You couldn't convince her before, what makes you think you can now?''

''Because you damn near broke her arm, you sonofa-bitch.''

''Is that what she told you?'' It was Andrews's turn to

laugh. "She fell. The woman's clumsier than a baby trying to walk."

Zach took a step forward, his mind reeling from the impact of Ron Andrews's all-too-familiar lies. "You and I both know that's not how it is."

"I don't know any such thing. But one thing I do know." Andrews pushed off the car and stood only a foot from Zach. "Beth is mine. She'll come back to me, like she always has. There's not a damn thing you can say to keep her from me. She won't listen to you, just like your mama never listened."

Fury raged deep in Zach's soul, and it took all his strength not to wrap his hands around Andrews's neck. "You're one sick bastard, Andrews."

"Think so?" A smirk replaced his grimace. "Well, why don't you do something about it? You look like you want to coldcock me, so why don't you?"

"Nothing would give me more pleasure."

"Then do it, Miller. Be a man, for once in your sorry life."

Zach clenched his fists at his sides. It would be so easy to throw a punch. But Andrews was on duty, and Zach couldn't afford an assault charge. "You'd like that, wouldn't you, Ronnie? You'd like to see my butt in jail so you could do whatever you wanted with Beth and Erin. But I'll see you in hell before I'll let that happen."

Zach turned and walked away but before he could get in the truck, Ron Andrews's parting words followed him like a stalker.

"You can't protect Beth, Miller. You couldn't before. You can't now. And that Barbie Doll you're pokin', she's going to see right through you pretty soon. Find out just how big a coward you really are. A man who sent his mama to the grave knowing she raised a pretty boy who couldn't take care of a woman.''

Zach wrenched the truck door open as the accusations hurled through his brain. And he pulled away damning the truth he found in them.

Erin was mildly aware of the weight pressing down beside her on the sofa. Her eyes snapped open. How could she have fallen asleep?

Relief washed over her when she realized Zach was sitting beside her, not Ron Andrews. With his shoulders slumped forward and his face in his hands, he looked as though he'd been through a war and lost.

Erin wrapped the blanket around herself and came to her knees. "Are you okay?"

His heavy sigh filled the room as he straightened. "Yeah."

She kneaded his shoulders, his muscles rigid beneath her fingertips. "You don't sound okay." She leaned around him and although the light from the double window was muted, she could see he bore no cuts or bruises. "You didn't shoot him or anything, did you?"

"No." He glanced at her dress draped over the coffee table, then pointed to the flannel robe resting over the back of the chair. "You can put that on."

"Okay." But she didn't move.

An uneasy stillness lingered. When Zach tensed, Erin dropped her hands from his shoulders and moved to his side. "Do you want to talk about it?"

"Not really."

"You need to."

He didn't look at her. "I need a drink."

"Not this time." She laid her hand on his arm. "Look, Zach, I want to know what happened."

"He denied it. End of story."

"Did you really think he wouldn't?"

Zach lowered his gaze to the floor and leaned forward again, his hands fisted on his knees. "I don't know what I expected."

"What did he say?"

"The usual crap, how Beth belongs to him. How if I didn't leave him alone he'd arrest me for harassment. How I couldn't—" Zach halted his words as if he'd reconsidered.

Erin wouldn't let him. "You couldn't what?"

"Protect Beth. Protect you."

His voice was full of remorse. Of guilt.

"He's wrong, Zach."

"He's right."

Erin laid her head on his shoulder. "No, he's not. You've done everything in your power to keep us safe. You couldn't prevent what happened at the apartment."

"I should have. I shouldn't have involved you in this mess in the first place."

"I became involved the day he showed up at the center."

Zach fell silent. Erin sensed he wasn't telling her everything. His wounds ran deep, and she was determined to get to the bottom of his pain, but she knew that would be no easy task. Right now she worried about his mental state and decided everything could wait until the light of day.

"Maybe we should try to get some sleep," she said through a yawn. "We'll talk more in the morning."

"I wanted to kill him."

The unexpected declaration startled Erin and caused her to sit up. "That's understandable."

Finally he looked at her, pain radiating from his dark eyes. "I could've done it. I wish I had."

Erin's heart went out to him. "And then you would have ended up in prison."

"I'm living in one now."

Erin swallowed around the knot in her throat. "There's more to this, isn't there?"

More silence.

"What are you not telling me, Zach? Does it have to do with Beth?"

His gaze slid away. "I could have stopped it. If I had killed *him,* then she wouldn't have suffered. But I stood by and watched."

"You did everything you could to try and help Beth—"

"Not Beth."

"Then who?"

"My mother."

Erin's breath caught as she realized Zach's emotional dam was beginning to burst, one fissure at a time. She braced for the revelations and prayed for strength to console him. "Someone hurt your mother?"

He rubbed his hands over his face as if trying to wipe away the memories. "Not just someone. My bastard of a father."

She'd never heard him mention his family before, apparently for good reason. "Your father beat your mother?"

"Yeah. With his fists. With words. Any weapon he could find. But he was a damn good doctor, or so they said. He healed the sick and tortured his wife. And while he basked in his pompous glory, I stood by and watched him tear my mother down bit by bit."

Erin's eyes misted as she tried to digest what he was telling her. "Where is your mother now?"

"Dead. My dad died first, from too much booze. I was thirteen. Mom died two years later from a broken heart." He released a humorless laugh. "She still loved the bastard even after all he'd done to her. I hated her for it, but I loved her, too. I used to have the fantasies about tying him up while he was passed out, then beating him with a baseball bat. Of course, I never had the guts to do it, but I imagined it all the time. Pretty crazy, huh?''

How many times had she heard similar stories from abuse survivors and their families? More times than she cared to count. ''No. Not at all. You were trying to cope.''

When she attempted to put her arm around his shoulder, he shrugged it off. ''So now you know, Erin. I've spent my life letting people down, especially those I care about the most.''

Erin suppressed a rush of anger and sadness, all rolled into one. She wanted to yell at him, to comfort him. ''You were a child, Zach. You had no control over the situation.''

''I failed her, dammit. Now I'm doing it all over again with Beth. With you.''

She framed his face with her palms. ''Beth is here. She's safe. I'm still in one piece. You're responsible for that.''

He shot off the couch and turned to face her, his voice full of frustration. ''For how long? How long before she goes back and Ron Andrews gets to you?''

''We won't let her go back. We'll find a way to stop him.''

''You can't stop her. Or him.''

She wouldn't let herself believe that. ''Even if that's true, that doesn't mean you've failed her.''

''God, I wish—''

Tightening the blanket around her with one hand, she rose to her feet and stood in front of him, reaching up to stroke his cheek with her thumb. ''What do you wish?''

He laid his hand on hers and turned her palm to his lips, giving her a gentle kiss. ''I wish I had your strength. I wish I had something to believe in, like you. I have nothing."

She really wanted to cry for him now, for everything he'd suffered through. All she could give him was comfort and compassion. "You have your business. You're helping the shelter. You happen to be the strongest man I know, Zach Miller. And I'm—" *Falling in love with you.*

The words came to her, so sharp, so clear, that she trembled. She didn't want to fall in love with him. He needed so much more than she could ever give him. He needed someone who was willing to give up her life for him. She could never be that woman. She wasn't sure if she could ever open her heart that wide again.

"You what?" he asked, pinning her with a questioning gaze.

She couldn't tell him. Not now. "I want you to forgive yourself."

"I never learned the meaning of the word."

"You have to, Zach, or you'll never get beyond this." She softly kissed his cheek. "Do it for Beth."

He sat and pulled her next to him, close to his side. "I'll try, but not for Beth. For you."

All Erin's emotions seemed to crash down on her at once. She fought back tears. She fought giving in to the love she felt for him at that moment. She fought opening herself to more heartache.

He smoothed the blanket from her legs and bent to place a kiss on her bare thigh. "I need you, Erin."

She didn't want him to need her, for fear she might start needing him. She couldn't need him. She would rather leave before all the hateful words, the sadness. Before he said goodbye. But they still had tonight. They both could use some comfort.

Erin slipped her fingers through his hair and cradled his

scalp as he rested his cheek on her leg. "I'm here, Zach." Then she leaned forward and kissed the back of his neck.

Zach slowly unwrapped the blanket the rest of the way, baring her flesh to his eyes and hands. She knew she should stop him; Beth could wake up and find them. But she also knew he did need to lose himself. Forget, if only for a while. She could give him that much.

By the time he had the blanket completely open, Erin gave in to the fire his appreciative gaze stoked within her.

"Zach, what about Beth?" she whispered. "Should we go into the bedroom?"

"No. I don't want you to move."

He took her lips with a passion she'd never before experienced. She tasted his desperate hunger, his overwhelming need. And for a moment she thought she tasted tears.

Suddenly he was on his knees before her, parting her legs to slip between them. He told her again that he wanted her, needed her, all the while plying her with tender kisses in the valley between her breasts, on her belly. He treated her like fine crystal, as if she might break.

Then he lowered his head and delivered a kiss so intimate, so earth-shattering, it took her breath. His hands seem to be everywhere, caressing her in ways she'd only imagined. He used his skilled mouth to play her like a fine instrument, focusing on her greatest need. And when a soul-wrenching climax overtook her, Erin's body shuddered in accord.

Zach lifted her up and positioned her on the narrow couch. After slipping off his shoes and socks in a rush, he tore at his shirt, cursing the uncooperative buttons. Once he shucked the shirt off, he withdrew a small packet from his slacks before stepping out of them and kicking them aside.

He stood before her, his beautiful body unveiled to her

eyes for the first time. Well-defined muscles graced his chest covered by a mat of dark hair. That hair created a path down his taut abdomen to his breath-stealing arousal, leaving no question in Erin's mind how much he desired her.

Every inch of him screamed all male. Undeniable strength. Absolute need.

Except for his eyes. Erin saw desperate hunger in their depths and raw emotion as naked as his powerful body.

He hovered above her for a moment, then slipped inside her willing body with a steady moan.

"I can't get close enough," he whispered, his words laced with frustration as he moved in long fluid strokes.

She tightened her arms and held him close, with body and soul. "I'm here," she whispered back.

"Don't leave me, Erin."

"I won't." Not tonight.

Tears slipped from her eyes as Zach slowed the rhythm and continued to whisper soft words in her ear, some endearing, some sensual, but all serving to make her want him more than she'd ever wanted any man. He touched her in ways she had never experienced, loved her with a passion she had only imagined. She gasped when another furious climax began to take over, racking her body with pleasurable spasm after pleasurable spasm.

With one long, hard thrust, Zach buried his face in her hair and muffled his cry, yet Erin could still hear the agony mixed with pleasure. She felt his pain as acutely as if it were her own, and wished she could take it all away.

After a few moments of silence in the aftermath, Zach raised his head. He studied her eyes, then said the words she was afraid to hear and didn't dare heed.

"I love you, Erin."

Zach knew in that moment he'd said the wrong thing.

He felt it in the way Erin's body tensed beneath him, her guarded silence.

He sat up and pulled her to his side. Still, she didn't respond. ''You think I've really lost it, don't you?'' he asked.

She reached across him and pulled the blanket over to cover them both. ''No.''

''Then for God's sake, tell me what you're thinking before I really do go crazy.''

She gave her hair a one-handed push away from her face. ''I think you just got caught up in the moment.''

He blew out a frustrated breath. ''You're wrong.''

''I also think you're mistaking gratitude for…deeper feelings.''

Damn! She couldn't even say the word. ''I've never told anyone I loved them, Erin. Not one woman, and there have been plenty.''

She toyed with the satin edging on the blanket, avoiding his eyes. ''I guess I'm flattered, then.''

''Flattered?'' The comment sent him off the couch to face her. ''That sure as hell isn't what I intended.''

Finally she met his gaze. ''What do you want me to say?''

He wasn't sure what he wanted from her. Maybe a hint that she had feelings for him, too. Maybe even denial. Something to let him know there was hope, or not.

''Why don't you start with telling me how you feel about me?'' he said.

''I care about you, Zach, but we've known each other for such a short time.''

''Maybe this is going to make me sound like an idiot, but I believe I've probably loved you from the first time I laid eyes on you. If that's nuts, then I'm totally insane.''

"You wanted me," she said. "There's a big difference."

He raked a hand through his hair. "Yeah, I can't deny that. But now I want more. I *feel* more."

She got up to retrieve the robe, while he slipped on his slacks. Once she was covered, she took a place on the sofa and huddled in the corner. "How much more do you want?"

He hadn't given it much thought, but the proposition made perfect sense. If she wanted them to have more time to get to know each other, then he'd give it to her. "Move in with me."

"I can't do that."

He expected she'd put up a fight. But he refused to back down until he heard all her excuses and dispelled every one. "Why?"

"First of all, Beth's here."

"She won't be here forever."

"Secondly, I have my own place."

"A place where you're not safe. A place that sits in the middle of a piece of property owned by your father, who, by the way, wants to control your life."

She sighed. "But the most important reason is I've done that before, and it doesn't work."

Zach remembered Gil telling him about her former boyfriend. He hadn't wanted to dwell on Erin's relationship with another man. He couldn't stand the thought of her being with someone else. The past belonged in the past. But if it meant finding out why she was so reluctant, he'd dredge up every last detail.

He sat back down beside her. "So you lived with someone before. That doesn't mean it won't work with us."

"This has nothing to do with him. It's me. I can't handle..."

Zach moved closer and took her hand. "You can't handle what?"

"The leaving part. I'm not good at goodbye."

Now he was getting somewhere. "Who says it will end in goodbye?"

"It always does."

Zach found himself growing angry with the man who had obviously shredded her heart, and he didn't even know the guy. "What did this Warren do to you?"

"Nothing I didn't ask for. I knew how he was from the beginning. Ambitious. Ruthless, almost. We met in college. When he finished law school, we moved in together. My father loved him, so much that he gave him a job. Two years later Warren found someone else. Someone who would make the perfect wife."

"You didn't fit the bill?"

"Not hardly." She raised her eyes to his, but he saw no tears or regret. "He still works for my father, as a partner now. My father blames me for the breakup. I wasn't willing to put my career on hold to be the consummate attorney's spouse, therefore I'm to blame. Once again, I disappointed him."

Zach shook his head. "For someone who's so headstrong, you put too much stock in your dad's opinions."

She shot him a scathing look. "And you didn't?"

He couldn't deny that. Regardless of how brutal his own father had been, many times he had sought his approval, without success. "Yeah, but you've made me see I need to get over my past and get on with my life. I can help you do the same. We can do it together."

He put his arm around her, but the way she flinched caused him to back off. "You won't even consider it?"

This time he saw regret in her blue eyes. "I can't, Zach. Not now. Not until I have more time."

"Fine." Zach stood and headed toward the bathroom, a deep ache settling in his chest.

"Where are you going?" Erin asked.

"To take a shower and get ready for work."

"It's not even close to dawn."

He faced her and steeled his expression. "Who can sleep? But you go ahead. Feel free to stretch on out and dream away. Personally, I've had my share of nightmares for one night."

Eleven

Erin woke the next morning to find Zach gone. She'd dozed on and off on the couch, although he'd again offered his bed. At one time she became aware of him sitting in the nearby lounge chair, watching her. She didn't dare speak, afraid if he persisted with his proposition, she might accept.

Now he had left her alone with an aching emptiness and a lot of food for thought. Wrapping the robe tightly around her, she sat up and pushed her tousled hair from her face, no idea what to do next, where to go. She needed to call her insurance company about the break-in. She needed to call Ann and tell her she'd be late. And she needed to find some clothes.

Shopping wasn't something she liked to do under normal circumstances, but she couldn't very well run around the shelter in a satin evening gown. She'd borrow something from the center's donated items. Now she knew how the residents felt when they left with only the clothes on their back.

The bedroom door opened, drawing Erin's attention. She'd almost forgotten about Beth.

Beth strolled into the living room, her face freshly scrubbed and her hair pulled into a ponytail. She looked at Erin and smiled. "Good morning. Where's Zach?"

Erin dropped her legs over the edge of the sofa, careful the robe stayed in place. "At work, I guess."

"You don't know?"

"I wasn't awake when he left."

"Oh." Beth took a dining room chair, turned it backward and straddled it. She rested her hands on the seat back. "I expected you two to be at your place. Or at least in the bedroom." She smiled a knowing smile as she eyed Erin's discarded clothes spread out on the table.

Erin shifted uncomfortably. "We couldn't stay at my place."

"Why not?"

Erin wasn't sure she wanted the responsibility of telling Beth about the break-in. If Beth decided to run, Erin probably couldn't stop her. But Zach could.

Beth narrowed her eyes. "Tell me, Erin. What's going on?"

Erin had no choice but to be candid. "Someone broke into my apartment last night. It was trashed pretty good."

"Ron." The name echoed like a gunshot in the apartment.

Erin drew in a cleansing breath. "We think so, but we're not sure."

"Did you report it?"

Although Beth hadn't said *him,* Erin knew what she meant. "I filed a report, but Zach didn't want me to name your husband yet. I wanted to, but he wouldn't let me."

Beth lowered her eyes. "I'm sorry. That's my fault. I told him I didn't want to get Ronnie in trouble. But it looks like he's doing that all by himself."

Erin scooted to the edge of the sofa. "He's totally out of control, Beth. We have to get you out of here."

"I need to go home. Try and calm him down."

"It's too late for that. It's time you stop protecting him. Let Zach call the police department before he hurts someone else."

Indecision warred in Beth's tired eyes. "I don't know what to do."

Erin stood, cinched the oversize robe tighter and took the dining chair next to Beth. "Yes, you do. It needs to be over, for your sake. For Ron's, too. He may have to hit rock bottom before he agrees to get help. Do it not only for yourself, but also for him. Before it's really too late."

Beth swiped away the tears trailing down her cheeks. She stared off into space, then looked at Erin. "Okay. I'll think about it."

Erin laid a gentle hand on Beth's arm. "If you'd like, I could call Ann and make the arrangements. At least find out what the next step would be in relocating you."

Beth nodded. "If it's not too much trouble."

Erin stood. "No trouble at all. First I need to take a quick shower and dress. I have to go to the shelter, anyway, so I'll talk to Ann then and have her give you a call."

Before Erin could turn away, Beth gripped her arm. "Thanks, Erin. For everything. Whatever happens, I appreciate all you've done."

Zach returned to the apartment after spending several hours staring aimlessly at a mountain of paperwork he had no desire to tackle. He could hear someone rummaging around in the bathroom and glanced at the clock. Almost nine. Beth had slept in. Good. She needed the rest.

The linens were folded neatly and resting in the corner of the sofa, evidence Erin had left. She'd probably caught a ride to the shelter just to avoid seeing him.

His thoughts came back to the night before when she had loved him so freely. But he couldn't get past her unwillingness to open her heart. Take a chance. And he wasn't sure if he should keep trying or say goodbye. After last evening's confessions, maybe she saw him as weak. Maybe she was right.

Tossing his sunglasses onto the dining room table, he decided he could use another cup of coffee. The lack of sleep in recent days had begun to catch up with him. He felt dog tired, but too restless to even try to catch a nap in his spare time.

After he made his way into the kitchen, he heard the bathroom door creak open.

"You want some coffee, sleepyhead?" he called.

"No. I have to head to the center. I'm late."

Zach froze, his hand poised on the coffeemaker.

Erin had been in the bathroom, not Beth.

He wasn't prepared to see her just yet.

He scooped the coffee into the filter, resisting the urge to go to her. Take her in his arms. Kiss her good morning. After he started the coffee brewing, he gave himself a mental pep talk and left the kitchen to face her.

She stood in the middle of the living room, dressed in the rumpled satin gown, toweling her hair dry. His heart nearly stopped at the image. In that moment he realized how tough it would be to forget her. To let her go.

"You look tired," he said.

She continued to dab at her hair with the towel. "I'll manage. Is Beth in the kitchen?"

"No. I thought she was still asleep."

"She was up earlier. She must've gone back to bed."

Dread spurred Zach into action. He strode to the bedroom and opened the door. Exactly what he feared. No Beth. He did find a note in the middle of the neatly made bed.

He grabbed the paper up and as he began to read, his chest contracted.

Zach, I have to go back to Ron. I'm afraid if I don't, all hell will break loose, and he'll come after you. I'd never forgive myself if he hurt you or Erin.
I'm sorry—Beth.

"Dammit to hell!" His shout brought Erin into the room.

She caught sight of the note in his hand, then her gaze snapped to his. "What does it say?"

He crumpled the paper and hurled it across the room. "She's gone back to him."

Erin placed a hand to her mouth. "Oh, God, no. How could she get past the guard?"

"She probably waited until shift change, then headed across the courtyard past the pool, out the back entrance. Besides, they were instructed to keep Ron out, not her in."

Zach dropped down on the edge of the bed and streaked his hands over his face. "You know what this means, don't you?"

She took a small step toward him. "What?"

"He's won again."

"And it's my fault."

He stared up at Erin, confused. "Why would you blame yourself?"

"Because I told her about the break-in."

Zach came to his feet and tried to stifle his frustration. "Why did you do that?"

"I thought I could convince her to move to Dallas. Instead she must have decided the only way to protect everyone was to go back to him."

Zach fished for the keys in his pocket and headed for the living room, Erin close on his heels. "I'm going after her, and I hope to God it's not too late."

Erin blocked the front door. "You can't do that."

"Watch me."

"If you do, you'll only make her resist that much more. She has to come to terms with this herself. But there is something you can do, although it's not without risk."

"What?"

"Let me turn him in."

Didn't she understand what Andrews was capable of? "No. If you do that, then he'll take it out on Beth. And you."

Erin studied him for a long moment. "When is it going to end, Zach?"

"I don't know." And he didn't. Right then he couldn't think, not with Erin staring at him. Waiting for him to make a decision. Waiting for him to do the right thing.

Without a word she brushed past him and picked up the phone to dial.

"What are you doing?" he asked.

"Calling Ann to come get me."

He released a breath of relief that she wasn't calling the department. "I can take you to the shelter."

"No. I need some time alone to think things through. So do you."

All the time in the world wouldn't help him. He had no idea what to do. Mentally and physically exhausted, he decided not to argue with her. "Okay. I'll call you later.

One of the guys will see you get there safely. And don't go back to the apartment yet.''

''I have to, Zach. I can't keep running. Neither can you.''

The following day Erin stood inside the door of the apartment with a cardboard box in hand and one of Zach's cronies hovering outside. Uncertain where to begin, she found herself moving toward the music box, the only thing of sentimental value she cared to salvage at the moment. Nothing else had been destroyed that couldn't be replaced. She knelt and gathered the pieces, one by one, trying hard not to let the tears fall.

''Erin, what happened here?''

She turned to see her father silhouetted against the door, a mortified look on his face. The one person she didn't care to see had found his way home in the middle of the day.

She stood and clutched the box to her chest. ''I'd like to tell you I had a wild party last night, but I'm afraid that's not the case.''

His gaze snapped around the room, then came to rest on her. ''Was it that man who's been threatening you?''

She shrugged. ''Possibly. But if that's who did this, we won't have to worry anymore.''

''Then he's behind bars, I take it.''

Actually, he was on the wrong side of the bars, something that made her physically ill. ''No. His wife's gone back to him, so he's probably a happy camper.''

''But you have no way of knowing that.''

''I know the type, Father. He's got what he wants, his wife, and he'll leave me alone.''

Robert took a step forward. ''Regardless, you need to move back in with me until they catch the perpetrator.''

She should have expected his suggestion. "No."

He scowled. "You're not considering living here, are you?"

"No, I'm not. I'm going to move into a town house. I put down the deposit this morning."

He assumed his politician posture, arms crossed over his chest, a look of concern on his face. "That's not necessary. I have plenty of room. I can watch over you."

Erin righted the club chair with one hand and dropped the box on its cushion. "You don't need to watch over me, Father. I'm way past the point of needing a nursemaid." Or jailer, for that matter.

He gave her an authoritative point with one sturdy finger. "You're not intending to move in with that security man, are you?"

She didn't need this. "And what if I am?"

"That would be improper."

Erin released a short laugh. "You didn't seem to mind when I lived with Warren."

"That's different, Warren was—"

"An ass. He didn't know the first thing about being kind and loving. Or romantic. I was his means of working his way to the top so he could grab the brass ring on the mother of all carousels. Brailey, Holder and Thompson. He's got *you* now. He never did want me."

"I believe it to be the other way around, young lady. If I recall, you were the one who broke the engagement."

"After he told me he wanted me to quit my job."

Robert let out a rough sigh. "Let's not rehash the past. Right now I'm concerned about your welfare. The security man isn't your type."

Erin felt her blood pressure rise. "It doesn't really matter if he is or isn't, we're not moving in together."

Robert's features relaxed. "Good. But you still need to

consider moving back in to the main house. If the truth be known, I've missed having you around to argue with.''

She picked the box up and shifted it to one hip. ''If you're that lonely, why don't you ask Warren and his new wife—Misty, I think her name is—to move in with you?''

When she noted her father's expression had gone from stern to sad, Erin felt an immediate pang of remorse. She knew how lonely he'd been since her mother's death. But as Zach had told her, being everything to him had been an incredibly large burden for Erin to bear. It was high time she thought about what she needed. Live her own life.

Still, she wanted to reach out to him, embrace him. But they hadn't hugged in such a long time. She wouldn't even know if he'd welcome that kind of gesture. Instead, she walked to him and laid a hand on his arm. ''Look, Father, I appreciate the offer, but my new place is only twenty minutes away. I'll see you every week at dinner.''

''I will hold you to that.'' He peered into the box. ''Is that the carousel your mother gave you?''

She followed his glance to the tattered remains. ''Yes, it is. It's ruined, I'm afraid.''

He met her gaze, a melancholy smile curling his lips. ''I remember when she gave it to you. She bought it in San Francisco while we were on a trip. A political rally. She took such pleasure in making you happy. Both of us happy.''

Erin's heart sank and her eyes misted. ''You really miss her, don't you?'' she said softly.

''Every day of my life. You're so much like her.''

Aside from physical appearance, she was nothing like her mother. ''I'm very much like you.''

Surprise passed over his face. ''Like me?''

Erin smiled. ''Who do you think told me that life wasn't worth living unless you had a cause? You did. I inherited my conviction from you. My strength. Why do you think we cross horns all the time?''

He paused as if considering her words. ''I suppose you're right.'' He laced his hands together in front of him and inclined his head. ''I can't talk you out of this?''

''No. Not this time.''

''This time? When have I ever talked you out of something you had your sights set on?''

She smiled in earnest. ''Come to think of it, never. But I got my stubbornness from you, too.''

He returned her smile. ''All right, then. And one more thing. Looks like your new shelter is well on its way to success. After calling in a few favors, J. W. Denton has pledged one hundred thousand dollars to the center in his mother's name. He only asks you name a room after her.''

Erin wanted to shout with glee. At least today turned out to have a bright spot. Who would have thought her father would be delivering the sunshine? ''Great! What's her name?''

''Minerva Wainwright Denton.''

''The Minerva Room it is.''

They stood for an awkward moment, staring at each other. He moved forward first and pulled her into an awkward hug. Erin wanted desperately to break down and cry, but she braced herself and simply enjoyed the moment.

He dropped his arms, and she gave him her best smile. ''Thanks, Dad.''

He looked a little misty himself. ''I can't believe it.''

''Believe what? That I thanked you?''

''No. That you called me Dad. I don't remember the last time you did that.''

''I'll try to do it more often. If you behave.''

He smiled. ''I'm proud you've done such a good thing

with this shelter, but I suppose it means you won't work for me.''

''I'll help out now and then.''

His smile turned to a frown. ''Promise me one thing, Erin.''

''What?''

''Be careful. It's a dangerous world out there.''

''Have you seen the living room furniture in the new place?''

Erin looked up from her work to find Gil standing at the door to her office, hands in pockets, looking at her expectantly. Almost two weeks had passed, and the shelter was coming closer to being finished, much to Erin's relief.

''No, I haven't had time to go by today,'' she said. ''I've got to check this grant.'' In reality she knew Zach was there, finishing up last-minute security details with two of his most-trusted men who would be assigned to guard the house upon completion.

Gil pulled up a chair in front of Erin's desk without being invited to sit. ''I don't know what kind of strings your father pulled, but the money's still rolling in. And the furniture's better than any I own. Actually, it's rather chic.''

Erin rubbed her temple, trying to thwart another headache, the second she'd had in as many days. ''It's probably some he had lying around since the last time he redecorated.''

''Well, wherever it came from, it's top grade.''

''Good.'' Erin shuffled some papers, hoping Gil would take the hint and leave. But he didn't move. He just sat and stared at her like she was some sideshow exhibit. ''Why are you here?''

''Just to visit. Thought you could use the company since

I haven't seen Zach around lately. Did you two have a lovers' quarrel?''

Great. This was all she needed, an in-depth discussion of her love life. "I'm sure he's busy."

"You don't know if he's busy?"

"Drop it, Gil," she said through clenched teeth.

"Whatever happened to his ex-partner?"

"She went back to her batterer."

Gil shook his head. "Another casualty in the war on domestic violence."

Erin seethed at the thought. She tossed her pencil aside and watched it roll off the desk. "We don't need any more casualties, dammit. We can't afford to lose one more woman. Someday this has got to stop."

"You can't save the entire world, Erin. You need to focus on those people you have helped save. Like Nancy Guthrie. She has a new job, a new apartment. Little Abby's safe."

Erin had been happy to learn that Nancy had done so well, but what about the others? Those that didn't prove to be a success story, like Beth Andrews? "If we lose one, then we fail them all. So don't tell me what I need to focus on!"

Gil put up his hands, palms forward. "Hey, I'm on your side, remember?"

Erin lowered her eyes in shame. "I know. I'm sorry. I'm tired. And stressed." She'd lain awake so many nights thinking about Zach. They'd talked over the phone several times, but not about their relationship. Obviously he'd decided she wasn't worth the trouble. Erin didn't blame him. But she did miss him. Too much.

"Understandable that you're exhausted," Gil said, breaking into her thoughts. "Ann's office couch isn't a great place to sleep. When are you moving back into your apartment?''

"I'm not.''

Gil laughed and rubbed his beard. ''You don't intend to stay at the shelter forever, do you?''

"No. The Colony Town Houses have an opening at the end of the week. I'll move then.''

Gil stroked his beard. ''No kidding? How does your dad feel about this?''

She didn't want to talk about that, either, but maybe she'd feel better if she did. ''He's not happy. But he wasn't happy about the break-in, either.''

"Have they caught the guy?''

"No, unfortunately not. They probably never will.'' Not unless Zach decided to do something about it.

A knock on the door drew their attention. She wasn't expecting anyone. She certainly didn't need any surprise visitors or board members.

"Come in,'' Erin said.

The door slowly opened, and there Zach stood, looking as gorgeous as the last time she'd seen him. And the time before that....

"Well, speak of the devil,'' Gil said, standing. ''We were wondering where you've been.''

"Around,'' Zach replied, but his gaze was locked on Erin.

"If you're looking for your money, the check's in the mail.'' Gil attempted a hearty laugh that died when Zach sent an annoyed look in his direction.

Zach brought his eyes back to Erin. ''I need to talk to Erin for a minute. Alone.''

"You don't have to tell me twice.'' Gil gave Zach a one-handed slap on the back and before he left said, ''I hope you can cheer her up. She doesn't appreciate my company.'' Then he exited, closing the door behind him.

Erin tried to calm her racing pulse and assume indifference. If she didn't, she'd be tempted to walk into his arms. ''What do you need, Mr. Miller?'' she asked with a shaky smile.

He took two strides toward her desk. ''You.''

That one word caused her heart to somersault in her chest. ''I assumed that's why you're here. So what can I do for you?''

''Have you thought any more about my proposition?''

''Have you thought any more about mine? What have you decided to do about Andrews?''

''I asked first. I know you've been living at the shelter, which can't be a great place for you to live. And now I'm all alone again with a king-size bed we've never used.'' He attempted a smile. ''You can move in anytime you want.''

''I don't want.'' Oh, but she did. It would be so easy to tell him yes. Call the complex and cancel her lease. She'd lose her deposit, but it was only money. Yet if she said yes to Zach, she would probably lose her heart. He had too many demons after him, and she wasn't strong enough to exorcise them. Besides, she was taking a much-needed step toward true independence. She needed to prove to herself that she could make it on her own, without any other influence. But that was only partly true. She was afraid. Afraid she wanted him too much. Loved him too much.

She sighed. ''I can't, Zach.''

He braced his hands on the desk in front of her. ''What excuse now, Erin?''

''I've rented my own town house. On the other side of the city. A nice place—''

"To escape?"

"That's not what I'm doing."

He straightened. "What about us?"

She honestly didn't know what to do about them. She hated the thought of not seeing him, but she needed time to mull things over. "I think maybe it's best we not see each other right now. I have a lot to do at Phase II. I don't have time for any diversions."

Zach swept his fist across the desk, knocking the papers onto the floor and startling Erin in the process. His expression melded into a mask of anger. "Is that all I am to you, Erin? A diversion?" He studied the ceiling as he paced back and forth. "Well, hell, and I thought we had something going on. I was stupid enough to think we cared about each other. Boy, am I an idiot or what?" He turned his back on her.

Erin hadn't expected him to react so strongly. She assumed he'd honor her wishes and let it go. Get on with his life. Warren had walked away without second thoughts, but then Zach wasn't Warren. "It's not necessarily forever. After the new shelter opens, we could get together for dinner and celebrate."

Zach faced her again, anger radiating from his dark eyes. "And have a quick roll for old-time's sake? I can't do it, Erin. I want all of you or nothing."

The tears came then, trickling down Erin's cheeks, rolling off her chin. She didn't bother to try and hide them. "You don't understand."

Zach slapped his palm onto the desk. "Then make me understand. Tell me what he did to you to make you close yourself off. Why you think I'd do the same."

She snatched a tissue from the box on her desk, hating her tears, her weakness. "I told you, it's got nothing to do with Warren."

"That's where you're wrong. It's got everything to do with him. And your dad. You just can't admit it to yourself. And until you do, you'll keep existing in this safe world you created. You'll run to Daddy when you need him, and you'll hate yourself for it. You'll try to find comfort in your work, and maybe you will for a while."

He leaned forward again, just inches from her, hands braced on the desk. "I tried that, Erin, and it's been a living hell. Until I met you, I kept myself safe by not getting involved with anyone. It's a terrible way to exist."

What could she say to convince him to leave it be? "Sometimes that's easier, Zach. Saves a lot of heartache."

The sadness in his eyes cut Erin's heart to the quick. "I tell you right now, Erin, it's going to be a lonely life. And one day maybe you'll think about what you could've had. What we could've had together."

He turned abruptly and headed toward the door. With one hand poised on the knob, without turning around, he said, "I really do love you, Erin. Crazy as it seems."

Then he was gone, taking with him another piece of Erin's heart.

On Friday evening Erin carried the last box into her new town house and plopped it down onto the dining room table. She looked around at the disarray and wondered how on earth she would find the time to put everything away. But at least it would give her something to occupy her mind. Something other than Zach and his parting words.

Much of what he'd said during their last encounter was true. Even though she was beginning to acknowledge that fact, she still had to come to terms with her lack of trust, her fear of letting go emotionally. At times she wondered if Zach could really help her in that respect. Other times she knew he could, if she could find the strength to let him.

What if she actually admitted she loved him, too? Was she ready to risk facing his rejection if he'd changed his mind?

He hadn't called again, and she had to accept the fact he was probably gone from her life for good. That acceptance gave her no peace.

With a sigh Erin moved on to the living room, deciding not to unload the kitchenware. She didn't intend to cook, anyway. Then she thought of Zach and the meal he'd made for them that had gone untouched while they'd spent the time touching each other. She thought of his easy laugh. His beautiful dark eyes. His hands that had loved her so completely.

Stop it!

Erin tried to shelve the thoughts along with the few keepsakes she'd managed to save after the break-in. So much had been destroyed the past few weeks, including her confidence. Half the time she questioned her decisions at the shelter, the other half she questioned her decisions of the heart. Mainly she questioned letting Zach go.

An odd shuffling sound drew her attention toward the kitchen. The short hairs on her head prickled. Her heart raced, and a shudder ran through her.

How silly, she thought. It wasn't the bogeyman—or Ron Andrews—who in her opinion were now one and the same. As Zach said, Ron Andrews had won, at least for the time being.

No more threatening phone calls. No more scathing letters. Nothing, only stark silence. Which almost frightened Erin more, not knowing whether or not he had beaten Beth on her return. Was she was now sitting at home, nursing her wounds and a shattered heart? Or was Ron in the "honeymoon" phase, swearing he wouldn't do it again, knowing in fact that he would when the time came? If only Erin could have done more.

A few moments passed, then Erin heard it again, a slow, dragging sound. Maybe even guarded footsteps.

You're just being paranoid, Erin. It's probably only the air-conditioning kicking in.

She glanced at the clock. Nearly 9:00 p.m. She needed to call Ann to check on the status of two new residents. Besides, she could use the sound of a friendly voice.

Skirting the boxes, Erin picked up the white phone hanging on the sofa table set against the living room wall.

No dial tone.

Dammit, just what she needed. The phone company had yet to turn on her line. Of all the stupid, idiotic, imbecilic...

The sudden noise behind Erin chilled her to the marrow.

"Hey, *Miss* Brailey, what's a nice girl like you doing in a place like this...all alone?"

Twelve

Zach sat alone tonight as he had for the past two weeks. He picked up the phone again, debating whether or not to call Erin. Gil had given him her new address and phone number, but only after Zach explained he needed to talk to her about the two guards he'd hired for Phase II. Still, he didn't have to call her at home. He could just as easily reach her at the center.

If he did make the call tonight, she would probably see right through him. She'd made it clear she didn't want him. He couldn't stand to hear her voice, knowing how much he still wanted her.

As soon as he faced the fact that she wasn't ready for any kind of commitment, he could get on with his life. Easier said than done.

Right now he needed to carry out his plan, the result of several sleepless nights and endless soul-searching. He couldn't wait much longer. He had to make the call that would start the bureaucratic wheels turning. Before Beth ran out of time. She might hate him for it, and things could get worse before they got better, but at least he could put an end to Ron's reign of terror. For a while. Then he would convince Beth to leave Ron for good, or at least give it his best shot.

Zach picked up the phone again and dialed the police department. He breathed a sigh of relief when he was told Madeline Wright, the chief of police, was still there. Hopefully she would understand why he'd waited so long to tell her about Ron Andrews.

"To what do I owe this pleasure, Zach?" Her tone was anything but light.

"It's about Andrews."

"What about him?"

"Maddie, he's not what he seems. For the past few years, he's been—"

"Beating his wife?"

Zach's chest constricted, and he had to struggle to breathe. "God, has he hurt Beth again?"

"Yes, but it wasn't too bad, relatively speaking. He knocked her around some. She fought back, got away and went to her sister's house. She came in and pressed charges against him this morning. They picked him up about an hour after that."

Zach wanted to shout with relief. Beth hadn't needed his help. Where before that might have made him feel like a failure for not being able to convince her, now it didn't. "I'm proud of her. Thank God she finally came to her senses."

"Why didn't you tell me about this sooner, Zach?"

"I promised Beth I wouldn't. And it had to be her decision, or she never would've left for good." It was exactly something Erin would say. She had taught him more than he'd realized. More than she would ever know.

He would call Erin after he hung up with Maddie and tell her the good news. Even if she didn't want to be with him, she'd want to know about this.

"Now if we can just keep Beth safe," Maddie said.

Alarms rang out in Zach's brain. "Maddie, please tell me he's still locked up."

"You haven't been gone *that* long, Zach. He posted bail about an hour ago. He's free for the time being."

Zach tightened his grip on the receiver. How stupid could he have been to think that Andrews would waste away in jail? "And Beth's still at her sister's?"

"Yes, but her brother-in-law assures me he won't let her out of his sight until they can get her relocated."

"Then she's going to move?"

Maddie sighed. "Looks that way. I called Dallas PD. They're finding a place for her to stay."

"Good."

"But I will tell you, Zach, Ron's loaded for bear. He's turned in his gun. He's suspended for now, and Internal Affairs questioned him for several hours. I don't know what he'll do. He's pretty much lost everything."

"And it's his own doing. I don't feel sorry for him."

"I'm not asking you to. I'm telling you to be careful. Your name came up several times, and when he left, he muttered something about going to find a Barbie Doll. Do you know what that's all about?"

Erin.

She was moving today. Had Andrews found her? If so, she would prove to be an easy target for his vengeance.

Zach silently vowed that he would die a slow death before he let Ron Andrews harm one hair on Erin's head. If he wasn't already too late. "Maddie, I'll call you right back.'' Without a goodbye he hung up and snatched the paper with Erin's address off the table, then headed out the door.

Grabbing his cell phone from the holder at his belt, he started dialing Erin's number before he reached the truck. It rang an interminable amount of time, but no one answered. He hung up and called again as he pulled out of the apartment.

If he hurried, he could make it to her town house in ten minutes. If he was lucky, she wasn't home. If he wasn't, Ron Andrews had already gotten to her.

''Damn!'' He tossed the phone into the seat when still no one answered. He could kick himself for not having Maddie send a patrol immediately while he'd still had her on the phone.

He dialed the department again and spoke with the dispatcher. ''This is Zach Miller. I need you to send a patrol to 1112 Randolph Drive. I'm on my way over there now.''

''That's in Briarsdale's jurisdiction.''

''Then call them, dammit. Get someone over there quick!''

''And the emergency?''

''Possible assault. Maybe even attempted murder.''

''Who's being assaulted?''

''The most important person in my life.''

He hung up with no more explanation in hopes that the dispatcher sensed his urgency. He could only hope he was overreacting and Andrews hadn't found Erin.

No telling what Erin would say if that were the case. She had made it clear as spring water she didn't want his protection, but right now he didn't give a damn. She could get mad as hell, rant and rave when he showed up, but it didn't matter. As long as he knew she was all right, he would take whatever verbal abuse she cared to dish out.

God, please let her be safe.

But when he pulled into the town house complex several minutes later, he realized his silent prayer had gone unheeded.

Parked at the curb behind the town house sat Erin's red convertible and Ron Andrews's truck.

Erin didn't have to look to know who stood behind her. Ron Andrews's voice was full of contempt and icy hatred.

She slowly turned to face him. He was leaning against the kitchen door leading to the patio, an evil smirk on his face.

Erin silently cursed her carelessness. In the process of unloading, she had made a grave error in judgment—she hadn't tripped the dead bolt on the kitchen door, allowing him entry without so much as a creak.

The sickening sound of the turning lock compounded her fear. With the exception of the main entry behind her, she was trapped.

Erin met his menacing glare head-on and attempted a smile. She refused to let him see her terror. "Did you come to help me move in, Detective, or are you a member of the welcoming committee?"

Without a word Andrews slipped his hands inside the pockets of his blue trousers. He was in the same dark suit he'd worn the first time she met him, which gave Erin little solace. But oddly she didn't see a weapon, yet that didn't mean one didn't exist in a place she couldn't see.

He glared at her and stood as still as a monument—a man with no principles or conscience.

"Well, Detective?" she asked, trying to control her shaky voice. "What do you want?"

His gaze darted around the room before coming back to Erin. "I want you to pay."

Her stomach pitched in time to her erratic heartbeat. "Pay for what?"

"For ruining my life," he hissed.

"You have your wife back."

"I don't have my wife back! Thanks to your meddling, I probably never will."

Maybe Beth had decided to leave permanently, Erin thought. Good. At least she would be safe from her husband's wrath. "Where did she go?"

He narrowed his eyes to menacing slits. "She's dead."

Erin fought the bile rising in her throat. "You killed her?" The words held a quality of hysteria, even to Erin's own ears.

"She's dead to me."

Erin didn't know if he spoke only hypothetically, or if in fact he had really hurt Beth. She would never forgive herself if the latter were true. Neither would Zach.

Zach, where are you when I need you?

But Zach wasn't here, leaving Erin to her own devices, all because she'd been too stubborn to listen to him. "Maybe you should sit down, Detective."

He grabbed up the high-back bar stool and flung it against the refrigerator. It bounced forward, nearly hitting Erin. An animal moan bubbled in her throat.

Andrews's bloodshot eyes bulged with fury. "Quit calling me that, damn you!"

Erin hugged her arms to herself and tried to stop shaking. "Okay, I'll call you Ron, then. If that's okay."

"No, it's not okay. I am a detective, but because of you and your boyfriend, that's over for me, too. Forever."

It suddenly became clear to Erin. Zach had turned him in.

Erin couldn't fathom that Zach hadn't called to tell her. Warn her. But then, he probably couldn't get through.

Wouldn't he have at least tried to come by? No. She'd made it quite clear she didn't need his protection on several occasions. And now she could very well suffer death by pride.

She drew a calming breath. "I'm sorry you're in trouble, but I'm sure if you agree to get help, you can get your old job back eventually."

His demented laughter filled the small space between them. "That's how much you know. You, Beth and Miller set me up. I won't ever work as a cop again. You're going to pay. All of you. But you first. I want Zach to see you after I get through with you. I want him to remember that, for the rest of his sorry life…if I decide to let him live."

Erin realized Ron Andrews was a hopeless case. Despite the fact that he'd finally reached the bottom, he wouldn't accept any guilt. Now he was out for revenge, and she would be his first victim if she didn't think of something quick.

"What if I talk to them?" she offered, trying anything she could to keep him talking while she planned an escape.

"You really don't get it, do you, *bitch?*" He took another stalking step.

What should she do now? Beg for her life? Cry?

No. She refused to give him the satisfaction of knowing he'd gotten to her. She would fight, no matter that she was no match for Ron Andrews under normal circumstances, much less in his current maniacal state.

"Why don't you let me call Zach, then you can talk to us together?" she asked.

He stepped closer. "You really think I'm a fool, don't you? Just like Beth."

"Beth loves you."

"Don't say that!"

Erin put her hands up in surrender. "Okay, we won't talk about Beth."

"You're right. I'm tired of talkin'."

He reached behind him. Erin backed up. She knew what he searched for, but that didn't lessen the impact of seeing the cold metal barrel of a gun glinting in the fluorescent kitchen light.

Her pulse pounded in her ears, and her palms began to sweat. She did a frantic visual search of the area. The living room door was to her back, the kitchen door to his. The only way she could escape was to run toward the front entry. He would probably shoot her in the back, but at least she would have tried to get away.

The sound of squealing tries drew their attention. Andrews grabbed Erin's arm and dragged her into the living room. With the gun at her back, he guided her to the picture window and yanked back the curtain.

The street stood empty and alone, exactly how Erin felt at the moment.

"It was probably just teenagers," Erin said, covertly eyeing the door handle only inches away from her fingertips. All she would have to do is reach out...

He poked the gun harder into her back. "You better hope that's all it is and not your boyfriend."

Then he turned her around and shoved her forward, away from the front door and her chance to escape.

Facing Andrews, Erin cautiously moved in front of the sofa, leaving the coffee table between them, affording her little protection. He smiled, an obscene grin full of contempt and loathing.

She lifted her chin, a sudden hatred replacing her fear. "You're really enjoying this, aren't you?"

His laugh reflected pure evil. "You're like a worm on a hook, squirming to get free. I could kill you now, but this is much more fun, watching you sweat. Just like I did in that jail cell before they let me go.''

From the corner of her eye, Erin caught sight of a flash of color moving in front of the living room window where the curtain had parted. Then she saw him.

Zach.

He'd come for her after all. But how could he get in? She forced herself to look away. She had to think and keep talking. Buy both of them more time.

''Can we at least sit down?'' she asked, glancing in Zach's direction now and then.

''I'm comfortable just like I am, but you can sit for a minute. Makes no difference to me if you die sitting or standing.''

Erin perched on the sofa facing the window while Andrews loomed above her, pointing the gun toward her head. He kept rambling on about the injustice of losing his job, her role in his demise, and began to rehash his history with Zach. The more agitated he became, the higher his voice rose—a grating pitch that revealed his delirium.

Erin was running out of time.

The appearance of Zach's face in the window, his gesturing, thrust Erin back into the fight for survival. He pointed toward the floor. As best she could tell, he wanted her to get down on the ground. Was he going to take a shot at Andrews? And if so, could the bullet completely penetrate Andrews and hit her? No, Zach wouldn't put her in more danger if he could prevent it.

Erin heard the faint sound of sirens and saw alarm in Zach's eyes. Andrews had yet to react, still continuing with his tirade as if he found comfort in the sound of his own voice. But it was only a matter of time before he heard the sirens.

As Andrews began to pace back and forth in front of the coffee table, Erin saw her one chance at escape.

She braced her hands on the edge of the table, where the heavy black sculpture sat in the middle, and called up every ounce of physical strength. If she could knock him off balance by pushing the table over, then she could possibly get away, or Zach could take his best shot.

Wailing sirens announced the police squad's arrival. With a curse Andrews turned his head toward the cacophony. "What the—"

Erin shoved the table, cutting the detective off at the knees, sending him backward. Shattering glass sliced through the room as Zach came hurling through the window. Erin hit the floor and rolled away to safety.

But one sound froze Erin in terror.

The firecracker discharge of a gun.

Zach opened his eyes to a sterile white ceiling and a god-awful chorus of blips and bleeps, enough noise to wake the dead. At least he was almost certain he hadn't crossed over into the hereafter. When he tried to turn to one side, a burning pain shot through him, confirming the fact he was still very much alive.

"Damn." His throat felt like sandpaper.

"Be still, Zach."

Zach turned his head to see his very own angel of mercy sitting at his bedside. Erin. Thank God she was safe. "Hey."

She smiled. "So you finally woke up. The doctor said you were pretty out of it in recovery. Do you remember anything?"

"Some. Not much until I arrived in the trauma room at the E.R. I remember riding up the elevator to surgery. After that, I woke up in recovery, and the doc told me the bullet didn't hit anything vital, and that I should be going home in a few days, barring infection. That's about it.''

''That's more than I expected you to remember.''

He focused on a white gauze bandage spanning Erin's cheekbone. He gently touched it. ''What's this?''

She expelled a ragged breath. ''Just a cut from the flying glass. I might have a little scar, but I figure that should give me character.''

God, he loved her even more than he thought possible. ''You have more character in your little finger than most people have in their whole being.'' He traced the outer perimeter of the bandage. ''Does it hurt?''

She glanced away. ''It's nothing. Really.''

Nothing? Any pain Erin had to endure wounded Zach tenfold. He guessed that was the curse of being in love. The scars he worried about most were those she would carry inside. He knew about those firsthand. If only she would let him help her get over them, the way she'd helped him. ''You're beautiful, scar or no scar.''

''Thanks for the vote of confidence.''

''By the way, that was a pretty gutsy move you made with the coffee table. Risky, but brave.''

''I had to do something.''

''I'm proud of you. You probably saved both our lives.''

She laid a hand against her chest and with mock surprise said, ''Little old me?''

He laughed. ''Yeah, little old you.''

She pushed a lock of hair away from his forehead. ''Do you remember the shooting?''

''Just bits and pieces. I remember tackling Andrews and the gun going off, but I didn't know if I was hit or him.''

''I assure you, Andrews is quite alive. The officers were right behind you. He's got a few cuts and bruises, but nothing compared to what he's dealt out.''

"And he'll be locked up for a long time. Attempted murder should carry a hefty sentence." Zach coughed, causing another shooting pain in his side. He flinched.

Erin feathered her thumb across his jaw. "I should probably go. Let you get some rest."

He captured her hand against his face. "Don't go yet."

"Are you sure?"

"Positive. I feel better with you here." Zach shifted again and tried to scoot up on the bed, avoiding all the tubes and wires. Again the pain in his side made him groan.

Erin shook her finger at him. "If you don't quit moving, I'm going to have to tie you down."

"Now that sounds like fun."

"At least you haven't lost your sense of humor."

Have I lost you? he wanted to say. So many unanswered questions still haunted him. So much he needed to tell her. But he felt too tired at the moment to go back over the same old territory. As far as he knew, nothing had changed. Still, he needed to tell her how he felt.

He curled his hand around hers. "Erin, I don't know what I would've done if anything happened to you."

She placed a fingertip on his lips to silence him. "I'm here, aren't I?"

"For how long?"

"Until you run me off." Her voice sounded cheerful, but her blue eyes misted. He could tell she had been crying before he woke up, and she looked as though she wasn't done yet. A single tear trailing down her cheek proved that theory.

He swiped it away with his thumb. "Hey, it's all over now. He can't hurt anyone anymore."

"It was a close call, Zach. I've—" She sniffed.

He hated to see her cry, and hated the fact he was in no shape to hold her. "You've what?"

She futilely tried to brush away another rush of tears. "I've been such an idiot."

Zach stroked her hair, his heart full of hope. "How so?"

"About Andrews. About a lot of things. The danger was real, and I was too stupid and too proud to listen to you. I almost got both of us killed."

It wasn't what he wanted to hear. He wanted to hear she'd been wrong about them. That she'd reconsidered moving in with him. That she loved him and just now realized it.

He squeezed her hand. "Like you said, we're both okay. No one could predict Ron would finally go over the edge."

"But you suspected he would all along."

"Yeah, but it doesn't matter now. All that matters is that you and Beth are safe."

She studied his fingers linked between hers. "I guess we can get on with our lives now."

"Yeah, we can." Although life without her was no great prospect. He wouldn't tell her that. She had to come back to him on her own. Not out of some sense of obligation or pity, but because she wanted to.

"I've been thinking about that," she finally said.

"Come to any conclusions?"

"One." She raised her eyes to his. "When they were loading you into the ambulance, I've never been so afraid in my life. All the things I wanted to say to you ran through my head. When they pulled away with you, I was so scared I'd never get the chance."

She drew a breath and released it on a sob. "I promised myself if you were okay, I'd tell you. And since you are okay, then here goes…"

She looked away for a moment, then turned her gaze

back to him. Zach held his breath in anticipation until his chest ached even more. But he wouldn't relax until she said her piece.

"What I wanted to tell you," she said, "is that I can't live without you. I don't *want* to live without you. I want to spend time with you and wake up every morning with you. But more important…I love you."

If Erin hadn't been holding his hand so tightly, Zach would have sworn he was dreaming. He started to speak, but she placed a fingertip to his lips. "Let me finish before I lose my nerve."

She inhaled deeply before continuing. "I want to know if your proposition about us living together is still open."

"No." The word slipped out without much thought. Although he was pushing his luck, he had bigger plans.

Hurt passed across her expression. She lowered her eyes and released his hand. "I guess I can't blame you for changing your mind."

He clasped her hand again and lifted it to his heart. "I said it wrong." She finally looked up, her heart in her beautiful blue eyes, giving him the courage to continue. "Yes, I want to live with you, but not *just* live with you."

She frowned. "I don't understand."

"Erin, I want to marry you."

Her eyes widened. "You mean like white-dress-buy-a-cake-throw-the-rice marry?"

Zach chuckled. "Or we could go small. Whatever you want."

She sat in silence for a moment. "No one gets married after knowing each other such a short time. People would think we're crazy. My dad would have a fit." She smiled. "I bet for the first time in his life, he'd be speechless."

Zach tipped her chin up with a fingertip. "I want your

answer based on how you feel about this, not on your dad's approval.''

Her smiled withered. ''I love you, Zach, and nothing my father says or does will change that.''

''So the answer is?''

''Yes.'' She laughed. ''Yes, Zach Miller, I'll marry you and live with you and drive you nuts on a regular basis.''

She bent and kissed him. Zach winced. She straightened, looking mortified. ''Did I hurt you?''

''The only thing that would hurt me at this moment is if you'd told me no.'' He slowly inched over and patted the bed next to him. ''Come here. I need you to kiss it and make it better.''

Erin stood, kicked off her shoes and curled up at his side. She toyed with the mat of hair on his chest exposed above the V-necked hospital gown. ''One question.''

''Yeah? Just one?''

She playfully swatted his good arm. ''Do you have a problem with my continuing to work at the shelter?''

''Wouldn't want it any other way.''

''You know, I really can't cook worth a darn.''

He kissed the tip of her nose. ''I can, remember?''

She grinned up at him. ''You are going to come in handy.''

''I try. And we have to have a honeymoon.''

''Hawaii?''

He grinned. ''I was thinking somewhere on a balcony.''

''Ah, you're finally going to fulfill my fantasy.''

''You bet. And there's something I need to ask you.''

''Okay.''

He worried she might change her mind after the next proposal, but he had to ask. In order to make Erin happy, he had to be completely satisfied with himself, his work. ''Would you object if I rejoin the force?''

She raised her head off the pillow. "Be a policeman again?"

"Yeah. I've been thinking a lot about it lately. I miss it, the beat, the challenge. Now that Ron's gone, I could go back. The job's waiting if I want it."

She sighed. "I'll worry a heck of a lot, but if it would make you happy, then that's what's important. But what about the security business?"

"I'll run it on the side."

Erin cleared her throat and fiddled with the plastic hospital bracelet on his arm. "There's something else I need to tell you, too."

"You have another man waiting in the wings?"

She frowned. "Not hardly. Beth was here a little while ago. She'll be back later. She's going to rejoin the force here in Langdon, too, since Ron's out of the way. Looks like you'll have your old partner back. She wanted to tell you herself, but I just couldn't wait. So act surprised, huh?"

Zach grinned. "I can do that. As long as you realize that Beth and I are only friends. I might spend my working hours with her, but it's you that I want to come home to every night."

She pressed another kiss to his lips. "You know, for a tough guy, you sure know how to say the right things to a girl."

If Zach lived to be a hundred, he'd never forget this moment, the joy in her eyes. "Have I told you that I love you?"

She smiled. "Not in the last couple of minutes."

"How stupid of me. Maybe I'll just show you."

They kissed in earnest then, with hearts and souls and, more important, with recognition of their love.

Zach felt a tug at his side and the material of the hospital gown lift away. Then Erin's long fingers skated across his belly just below the bandage in featherlight strokes, as if she could heal him with her beautiful hands. He supposed she probably could. She was doing a pretty good job of getting his mind off the pain.

He broke the kiss and said, "Are you trying to seduce me, ma'am?"

She pulled the gown up and peeked beneath it. "Just checking out your bandage. It covers a lot of area and— oh, my, looks like something else is coming into view."

Zach wiggled his eyebrows when she grinned up at him. "I think you stirred up trouble, Ms. Brailey."

"I think I'm glad everything's working, Officer Miller."

"That's Sergeant Miller, ma'am. At your service, cocked and ready." Zach pulled her closer. "Do you realize this is the only time we've been in a bed together?"

She worried her bottom lip. "You know, you're right."

"Yeah, and we might as well put it to good use. No telling what the room rate is around here."

Erin gasped when he cupped her breast. "We're in a hospital, Miller. Not to mention it's broad daylight, and you've recently been wounded."

"Why should we care about someone catching us?"

"You're right. I only care about us. Being with you. Spending forever with you, starting now."

"In that case you'll never have to worry again. You've got me forever."

To Erin forever didn't seem like nearly enough time.

*   *   *   *   *

SILHOUETTE® *Desire*

Get ready to enter the exclusive, masculine world of the...

TEXAS
Cattleman's Club

Silhouette Desire®'s powerful new miniseries features five wealthy Texas bachelors—all members of the state's most prestigious club—who set out on a mission to rescue a princess...and find true love!

TEXAS MILLIONAIRE—August 1999
by Dixie Browning (SD #1232)
CINDERELLA'S TYCOON—September 1999
by Caroline Cross (SD #1238)
BILLIONAIRE BRIDEGROOM—October 1999
by Peggy Moreland (SD #1244)
SECRET AGENT DAD—November 1999
by Metsy Hingle (SD #1250)
LONE STAR PRINCE—December 1999
by Cindy Gerard (SD #1256)

Available at your favorite retail outlet.

Silhouette®

If you enjoyed what you just read,
then we've got an offer you can't resist!

Take 2 bestselling love stories FREE!
Plus get a FREE surprise gift!

Clip this page and mail it to Silhouette Reader Service™

IN U.S.A.
3010 Walden Ave.
P.O. Box 1867
Buffalo, N.Y. 14240-1867

IN CANADA
P.O. Box 609
Fort Erie, Ontario
L2A 5X3

YES! Please send me 2 free Silhouette Desire® novels and my free surprise gift. Then send me 6 brand-new novels every month, which I will receive months before they're available in stores. In the U.S.A., bill me at the bargain price of $3.34 plus 25¢ delivery per book and applicable sales tax, if any*. In Canada, bill me at the bargain price of $3.74 plus 25¢ delivery per book and applicable taxes**. That's the complete price and a savings of at least 10% off the cover prices—what a great deal! I understand that accepting the 2 free books and gift places me under no obligation ever to buy any books. I can always return a shipment and cancel at any time. Even if I never buy another book from Silhouette, the 2 free books and gift are mine to keep forever. So why not take us up on our invitation. You'll be glad you did!

225 SEN C222
326 SEN C223

Name	(PLEASE PRINT)	
Address	Apt.#	
City	State/Prov.	Zip/Postal Code

* Terms and prices subject to change without notice. Sales tax applicable in N.Y.
** Canadian residents will be charged applicable provincial taxes and GST.
All orders subject to approval. Offer limited to one per household.
® are registered trademarks of Harlequin Enterprises Limited.

DES00   ©1998 Harlequin Enterprises Limited

In March 2001,

✦ *Silhouette*® *Desire*®

presents the next book in

DIANA PALMER's

enthralling *Soldiers of Fortune* trilogy:

THE WINTER SOLDIER

Cy Parks had a reputation around Jacobsville for his taciturn and solitary ways. But spirited Lisa Monroe wasn't put off by the mesmerizing mercenary, and drove him to distraction with her sweetly tantalizing kisses. Though he'd never admit it, Cy was getting mighty possessive of the enchanting woman who needed the type of safeguarding only he could provide. But who would protect the beguiling beauty from *him…?*

Soldiers of Fortune…prisoners of love.

✦ *Silhouette*®
Where love comes alive™

Available only from
Silhouette Desire at
your favorite retail outlet.